CONTENTS

Forbidden Lessons

Sexy Stories Collection

VOLUME 48

11 EROTIC SHORT STORIES

CARLEE SHOMAN

CHANEY KEES

Publisher's Note: This is a work of fiction. Names, characters, places, and incidents are a product of the author's imagination. Locales and public names are sometimes used for atmospheric purposes. Any resemblance to actual people, living or dead, or to businesses, companies, events, institutions, or locales is completely coincidental.

Forbidden Lessons/ Carlee Shoman, Chaney Kees. -- 1st ed.
Xplicit Press, an imprint of TLM Media LLC

ISBN-13: 978-1-62327-579-2
ISBN-10: 1-62327-579-2
eISBN: 978-1-62327-629-4

Printed in the United States of America

1 THE APPETIZER

I finally got home from work and I'm exhausted. I enter the house to find you at the stove, mixing a pot of something, a jumble of food and utensils scattered on the counter.

"Hello Brenda, hello mess," I introduce myself as I shut and lock our apartment door.

You turn to look at me with a sheepish smile on your sweet face, a silent apology for your aptitude at making a mess. I remove my large hairclip so my long red locks can flow freely over my shoulders, tips reaching my breasts. I kiss your cheek softly and survey the homemade soup you're working on and the grilled sandwiches on the next burner in a covered pan.

"Mm, yummy," I grab your tight little ass, only sort of referencing the food.

"How was work?" you ask sweetly as I step out of my heels and hang up my jacket, revealing that white button-up shirt you love.

"It was okay," I reply absently as I pour myself a glass of ice water. "Sure could use a nice massage after dinner," I reply with a sly grin. You turn again to look at me, eyebrows raised. "I just requested an innocent massage!" I defend quickly.

"You asked for a not-so-innocent rub down after dinner, which would be followed by an even less innocent dessert." Your eyes are flat as you pretend to be entirely not amused. I grin and quietly nod, liking the sound of this. You roll your eyes at my reaction and again turn back to cooking, adding chopped celery to the pot of simmering soup.

I set the glass down and cross the kitchen, put my hands on your waist and press my hips against your finely shaped butt, nuzzling my lips against your warm, bare neck. I feel you press your ass against me the slightest bit, tilt your head away so I can kiss you more. I sniff you softly so that I can smell the sweat from a hard day sweetly coating your caramel skin. I moan a sigh and kiss again so you can feel the vibration of my vocal chords in that sweet spot above your collarbone.

You set the burner for the pot on low and switch the burner for the sandwiches off completely before melting into me.

"Why don't I finish cooking later," you say weakly, words broken and a tension-filled silence following your request.

"That's a good idea," I exhale against your ear, warmth flooding between my legs.

I notice how tight my jeans have gotten, sticking to my skin with a sudden flush of sweat. I lock our fingers and lead you into the living room. You lie on the couch and look up at me with wide eyes, nervous but inviting. I straddle your waist, a knee beside each of your womanly hips, and lean down to kiss you. At first slowly, mouths closed, secretly hungry but very well contained. But the hunger deepens because of how desperately I want you; trying to contain myself only makes the desperation increase. I turn my head towards the back of the couch and you quickly press your soft lips against my ear, your breathing softly labored and hot on my skin. You kiss me and allow a quiet moan to escape you, then suckle at my neck. I sit up, gently grinding on your waist, and remove my shirt. My red curls fall back into place, a stark contrast against my pallid skin and enhancing the freckles that cover my cheeks, my arms and chest and delicate shoulders. You take in the image before you with eyes wide again, observing how the freckles are dark and plentiful just beneath my neck, on my collarbones, and lighten and thin as they reach the fringes of the cups of my blue bra. You place your warm hands on my waist, and goose bumps break out across my exposed stomach. You graze my hips, move to the top of my butt and raise your hands to admire the dimples of my lower back. You raise your hands until they find my bra clasp. I lean forward so you can reach better, pushing out my cleavage so that it swells within and over the cups. After a moment, you unhook the catch and release my breasts, ease the straps from my shoulders and toss my bra onto the floor. Your hands roam my newly exposed skin, cupping my tits, tracing circles around my nipples. I'm hard, almost immediately and I close my eyes, enjoying the incredible sensation of the air in my chest, enjoying being exposed and vulnerable to you.

"Your body," you whisper.

I watch your thick lips move as you slowly speak. I yearn for them to press again on my skin in even more intimate areas, wet kisses on my chest, tracing my areolas with a sly tongue so they further harden, skin bunched like a round little maze, a secret code. I yearn for you to drag your moist lips and tongue down to trace the slight silhouette of a six-pack on my abdomen and then lower, nearing my hipbones and the slight valley between them, then lower.

I lean down over you so our bodies are parallel, waists no longer touching. You admire the way the light from the windows brightens some parts of my skin, projecting shadows on other parts, like on my neck and below my breasts. "What about my body?" I ask, making my voice sexy and smooth; I lower my right breast close to your face, let my hardened nipple graze your lips.

"I want it," you moan, your tongue tickling my nipple as you speak. "I want you, Cara," you admit, voice a groan, deep and hungry.

I shift so my knees are at the sides of your ribs. You unbuckle the button of my black pants and slowly unzip them while looking into my eyes longingly. You can smell my wetness, I know. I grind on top of your breasts the slightest bit, my arousal increasing exponentially. I stand up and wiggle out of my jeans to reveal tight little booty shorts. I turn around so you can see how they ride slightly between my ass cheeks. I bend over as I slowly lower my panties, ensuring that the wetness in the crotch of them is visible to you. I step out of the panties and urge you to sit up on the couch. I sexily remove your shirt, then your workout bra to reveal your voluptuous DD breasts that I can't get enough of. I sit on your lap and take one of them into my mouth, teasing the other with my hand. I struggle to stifle a moan, feeling their weight against my palm and their simultaneous fragility against my teeth.

I urge you to stand, and then get down on my knees. I look up at you while I unbuckle your jeans; slowly peel them from your sweaty skin. I let them stay hooked at your ankles, and then begin toying with your panties. You're wearing cheekies, the cute red superman-themed ones that I love. I shift closer and hug around your waist, my cheek against your crotch and hands grabbing at your voluptuous butt. I can smell your arousal soaking at the cloth of your panties, and it makes my mouth water. I lower the underwear very slowly, past your muscled thighs, strong calves. I help you step out of your jeans and the now-moist cloth, and direct you to sit down again on the couch. You sit normally, shoulders against the back of the couch and feet on the floor. I straddle those strong thighs, knees against your hips, and I kiss you passionately. It's been a long day filled with teasing texts about how much you miss me and how great last night was.

I enjoy the amazing feeling of our nude, goose bumped bodies pressing together as we kiss. Our breasts are touching and our pussies are close, but not quite close enough, yet. I grind slowly on your lap while we kiss, feeling the hint of my wetness spreading towards my thighs and on your skin with my movement. It arouses me further, knowing such private secretions are dripping directly between your legs. I moan into your lips while we kiss, tongues wrestling and dancing, gaining velocity and pressure as our desires heighten. I pull away from your lips and pant into your neck, out of breath but energized and desperate. "Brenda," I moan in agony. "I need you, now."

You quickly shift and sit up, pressing my back onto the seat of the couch. You slide down and begin caressing and kissing my breasts. You kiss my lips for half a moment, then move to my cheek, my ear, my neck. You follow my collarbone with your tongue, then kiss the freckles on my chest before greeting my nipples again. I squirm in agony, desperate for release. You take your time, catching my eye occasionally and smirking at my impatience.

Your hands grip at my sides just the

way I like, nails digging just enough to leave weak imprints on my supple skin. You lower further, kissing and licking below my breasts. You begin to kiss all over my stomach, making me shiver. Goose bumps break out on my skin with the too-soft sensation. You tease me wittingly, kissing very low, near my hipbone, making me think you're going to give in to my desperation, then rise again to kiss near my belly button ring.

"Pleeeeease," I moan, gritting my teeth. I feel my secretions dripping from me.

"Okay," you reply simply with an eye-locking look and a soft smile.

You lower further and spread the lips of my pussy, which is puffy and engorged with blood from the arousal. You kiss just above my slit softly and sweetly, then lick your lips and kiss again in the same place. You pull back to admire the slight wet mark you've left on my recently shaven skin. I squirm in dissatisfaction, greedy for something more.

"Patience," you whisper.

I buck my hips at this utterance, raising myself closer to your lips. You immediately lean in and give my wet lips a kiss and I let my hips drop, surprised. You giggle at the surprised look on my face and I whine of desperation and embarrassment of my desperation.

"Please just fuck me," I beg.

You smile, rise to kiss me long on the lips, ignoring my hungry tongue pressing at yours. You lower again and settle yourself between my nervous legs. You kiss the inside of my upper thighs, letting the tip of your tongue dance just next to my labia majora. I can't contain myself; I grind against your face and you pull away slightly but maintain direct contact. You kiss my outer lips, then take them one at a time in your mouth and suckle. You let your tongue slide between my labia majora and minora, licking at my more sensitive nerves. You shift upwards slightly to kiss just above my pulsating clitoris and I grip at the edges of the couch cushions. You lower to kiss my clit then suckle on it gently. My hips buck and legs quake, overwhelmed with the intense pressure and pleasure on such sensitive nerves. You hum softly with your tongue against my clit, letting the vibrations tease me silly. You begin licking at me, tasting the wetness around my hole. I grind at your lips again, wanting the attention concentrated on my clit. I'm not far from orgasm. You know this. But you enjoy the tease. You relish in the potent taste of my fresh secretions before returning to my clit. I grab at your hands with mine and hold you tight within my fingers as the sensation quickly becomes unbearable of you sucking at my clit, tracing over it with my tongue slowly at first, and then more quickly, developing our usual rhythm. I grind on with the movement, moving against you to increase the pressure, moaning. "Baby," I exhale, feeling the arousal increasing exponentially between my legs, feeling my legs quivering, the arousal taking over my entire body. You move your tongue faster in response and the orgasm begins. You suck harder and move your tongue more quickly and my body explodes with the overwhelmingly pleasurable stimulation. My limbs erupt with tremors and my breathing, already labored, becomes shallow. "Oh, baby..." I say softly as the orgasm commences. Your tongue movements slow, then you rest with your lips against my still-pulsating clit. You enjoy the contractions. After a moment, you crawl up my body to lie against me and I curl into you, exhausted and almost high with the endorphins rushing through my system.

"I bet you're hungry," you say after a few minutes with a slight smile. I grin sheepishly in response. "We're going to eat naked tonight," you say happily, as you rise to turn the stove burners back up to finish cooking. I relax on the couch a bit longer until I can smell the food strongly, and my stomach growls. I look at you, embarrassed at the loud noise. You eye me and chuckle. "It's almost done, get in here."

"Okay," I reply happily, bouncing into the kitchen. I look over the food still on the stove before getting out the dishes and smack your voluptuous ass, just once.

"Later," you reply flatly, with sarcasm.

"Fine," I whine in return, setting the table. You pull me over for a nice kiss.

2 KESTREL'S LESSON IN SUBMISSION

The night air is warm and scented with the acrid sweet combination of jasmine and car exhaust. It is a fitting smell for the night and the things that lay beyond the plain door that the nervous woman stands in front of. Her hands shake as she pulls the paper she printed out from her computer out of her purse. The digital age has invaded even the alternative lifestyle, and the irony of it does not escape her. The trembling page is a one-night membership form to the dungeon she is in front of and trying to get up the courage to enter.

She has wanted this for a long time, ever since she stumbled across a porn site where she watched, wide-eyed and breathless, a woman tied down and spanked before being fucked, and fucked hard, by another woman. She had sat there at her computer with her breath heaving in and out and her fingers squirming against her clit for nearly an hour, her body seemingly unable to stop its lustful demands.

She thinks back to the moment when she had begun to research about the sex she had seen on that screen and what the language meant; the questions she had had to ask herself: Do I want this? Is this crazy? All she had known for certain was that the sight of rope around wrists and ankles and the sound of a hand striking a bare ass had made her pussy incredibly wet.

More porn had followed and she had begun to buy books that featured stories that had that type of rough sex in them. She read them helplessly and with avidity that she could not even describe. The images haunted her. She would find herself pulling on her own hair, biting her arm, and twisting her nipples viciously while she masturbated. She had no longer cared, by then, if it was right or wrong; she had only known that she wanted it—and she wanted it very badly.

A few weeks ago, she had stumbled across a small clue in a group she had joined. The group had open discussions on the subject, and there was a button to click on if anyone wanted to attend a dungeon event. Her fingers had shaken mightily as she had hit that button.

"You've come this far," she scolds herself as she stands in front of the door. "Do not go chicken shit now. It is all in there, behind these doors. The whole thing, every single thing you want. You know you want it." She does want it. Her pussy feels heavy and full; slickness is seeping from the pink slit of it into her panties.

Kestrel finally finds her nerve. She reaches out, pushes the bell, and waits for the door to wheeze open to allow her to come in. She blinks and shivers in the tiny hallway that leads to an arched doorway. From some shadowy distance, screams and moans sound out. She gasps in sudden arousal, her thighs giving off a slick little quiver, and she can feel the lower part of her belly turning into liquid.

"You got a membership?" The dungeon monitor asks her. She hands over the paper, five dollars, and her ID. The monitor takes it and points to a series of plain clear plastic totes stacked neatly on one wall. "Ten bucks for rental to stash your shit here."

She hands over the cash and her purse, and then she steps out of the little black dress, equally proper attire either for cocktail parties with your husband's boss or for getting your kinky rocks off. To show up in fetish wear is fine; to show up naked is also accepted. The dungeon sits in the middle of a long block of buildings in a rusting and mostly abandoned industrial park in the lower southeast, where the recession took a heavy toll. There are no passersby and no other businesses that are open, and the sounds coming from the rooms in the dungeon get lost in the vast maze of brick and forgotten heavy equipment. Her biggest fantasy is to show up naked, to be dragged outside, and to be fucked on the hood of a car in plain view of any and everyone who should choose to look. It is something she is working up to.

The monitor is a tough old dyke with a long graying braid, rabbity pink-rimmed eyes, a hawk-like nose, and a stick-thin body that is clad in all black except for the bright yellow and green vest she wears. Everything about her screams wannabe '50s style hood. Kestrel knows by looking at her that she wears a stinking, creaking old leather jacket; used to ride or still rides a motorcycle; and is possessed of that arrogant and thickheaded cunning that seems to come with the territory that makes up that certain type of dyke.

The monitor gives the hot figure sub a long look, but the sub ignores her. It pisses the monitor off but she is there to watch, not get off, and if the sub before her is unwilling, so be it.

"Don't know what you're missing, bitch," she thinks, and the sub tosses her lustrous black hair over her shoulder and walks into the dark.

Scenes are being played out everywhere. The dungeon is pansexual and she watches a pretty woman who is dressed as a little puppy being let off her leash and ushered into the kennel that sits on one side of the long front room. The puppy barks joyfully and begins to wrestle and prance around with the other humans dressed as puppies that are already in the pen while their indulgent owners watch with small grins.

A man is strapped to a Saint Catherine's cross and she stops to watch as he is beaten by his male top. A stern-faced man walks past with his large and erect cock jutting out in front of him and his sub crawling alongside. Kestrel can feel her thighs becoming slick and glassy with the proof of her desire, but she is searching for one particular thing.

Two women watch her restless prowling. They both make the move at the same time and the three of them wind up standing in the same space. Kestrel knows

Dommes when she sees them and she drops her head, letting her hair swing forward, and waits to see who will take her.

There is a moment's pause, and then one of the Dommes, a luscious redhead wearing a painted-on latex cat suit that outlines every dangerous curve, every high arch of breast and ass, says in a bored voice, "No, really, you take her."

The second Domme is a pretty, slightly thick woman with long red-gold hair, a rather unusual tattoo of musical notes and bars that angle across her entire forearm and collarbones, broad hips, and a set of firm breasts that are shown off to their best advantage in the crotchless one-piece fishnet outfit that she wears. Her eyes are stern and her demeanor hard. Kestrel wants her instantly. She also wants the ridiculously sexy redhead. She stands there torn and waiting with her body moist and the urge to get on her knees and beg for one of them to want her becoming harder to ignore.

"We could both take her."

Those words cause Kestrel's crotch to flood with heated oil. Her breath catches and her head jerks up, her excitement causing her to forget her place.

"What are you looking at?"

Kestrel immediately drops her head, anxiety whirling in her belly, and she hopes she has not blown the whole deal. The idea of it is too much; she is awash in lust.

"Hmmmm...," the redhead purrs and tilts one hand under one of Kestrel's milky white breasts. They are small and well made; they lay against her thin rib cage. She knows her concave belly, long legs, and small ass make her attractive, but what she doesn't know is if those will be enough.

The other woman taps Kestrel on her ass lightly with the tip of one finger; her long red nail taps and then scratches, and the heat blossoms and spills over. Kestrel cannot stand it any longer.

"Please Ma'am," she whispers, "I want to serve you."

"She wants to serve us," the redhead mocks, and tears start to run down from Kestrel's eyes and spill down her cheeks. Her breath grows short and her legs weak as they shove her back and forth between them, laughing and prodding at her flesh. Fingers slide wickedly across her fevered flesh and she bites her lip hard enough to bring blood to keep herself from begging again.

"Hard limits?"

Kestrel looks up and a smile erases her tears. They are going to allow her to serve, and she knows it. She stutters out her list. They ask for a few things, they talk for a while, and eventually there is an end to the negotiations and they move to a small room at the end of the hall that is currently unoccupied.

The redhead carries her tools on her belt. The sight of them there makes Kestrel want to melt—a small warm-up flogger made of deer hide, a one hundred fall flogger, and a riding crop with a stinger tip. She wears a harness and a huge black strap-on resides in it. That makes Kestrel dizzy, the sight of those womanly curves and that manly length.

The other woman carries a small pack on her back. She opens it to reveal a supple leather belt, a set of wrist and ankle cuffs, a short spreader bar, a black silk rope that has been neatly cut into long lengths, an anal hook, clothespins, and a blindfold. She takes out her own harness; the slapping of the buckles makes Kestrel shudder all over, and she cannot take her eyes off of them as they stand there posing and forcing her to see just how deep they are going to be inside her body.

Looking at the easy way they move together, she realizes this is not a new scene to them; they have co-topped before. Her heart thunders and shudders as the redhead says, "I am Mistress Summer and that is Mistress Winter; we are the season bitches, and you will see how much you like hot and cold before you get to go home tonight. You will behave little girl, or you will be sorry, do you understand? You will do what you are told and only what you are told to do, are we clear?"

"Yes, Ma'am," Kestrel says meekly.

"Who gave you permission to speak?"

It was a trap and she had not seen it. Her eyes flicker back and forth, but there is no mercy from either Domme. Mistress Winter forces her to turn around, to bend over, and to grab her ankles, and she does so. Her back stretches and her hamstrings let out a small gasp of misery while a hard hand slaps across her ass cheeks, softly at first and then harder. She squirms and wriggles but does not try to stand upright—to do so would invite more punishment.

"What is this?" Mistress Winter asks as she thrusts her sticky glove-coated hand under Kestrel's nose and rubs it into her face. "Did you cum while I was spanking you? Did you fucking cum without my permission?"

She wants to lie but she will be punished if she does. She wants to lie because she knows she is going to be punished for that. If she tells the truth, she will be punished for cumming when she did not have permission to. Either way, she wins. She might as well tell the truth then. Her stomach drops and a rush of endorphins lifts her high. Her blood buzzes in her veins and she whispers, "Yes, Ma'am. I came without your permission."

"Come here." Mistress Summer grabs her and drags her across the cold and stingy room; the concrete floor is crumbled and broken in spots, causing her to stumble and nearly fall. Her ankle twists in her high-end stilettos and the Domme growls out at her, yanking her arm and keeping her upright.

Mistress Winter is an expert with rope. She binds Kestrel's breasts first, looping the strong and soft quarter-inch nylon rope around each breast, flicking the sweetly pink nipples with her thumbs and tongue, pinching and biting just hard enough to bring blood to the surface but not to break the skin. Kestrel's breasts are bound into rounded globular shapes and the rope tugs and pulls, causing an unbearable want to hit her crotch.

"Thank you, Mistress." She whimpers and the woman looks at her with a mocking sneer, slaps her lightly on her cheek, just enough to sting, and replies, "You are going to be sorry for speaking to me."

Her arms are cuffed. The cuffs are roped together and yanked high overhead. She dangles there, and her feet are barely able to touch the floor, her weight hanging from the rope and the hook. The pressure is painful and she feels fear crawling and sliding, but her crotch is wetter than ever and she watches with lustful eyes as Mistress Winter cuffs her ankles and spreads her legs apart with the long steel bar that attaches to the cuffs.

The flogger is a small one that has enough softness to keep it light but enough bite to give it a sting. Mistress Summer uses it well, throwing from her wrist and forearm, not lunging forward, tracking the tails like only an experienced player can. There is a soft whistle as the tails fly, a hissing cut of the air. Kestrel leaps and dances, and her breasts sting slightly and begin to redden. This is a warm-up, not a beating, and she begins to quiver and moan as Mistress Winter joins in the fun with scratchy scouring pads, rubbing the dark-green things over Kestrel's ass and giving her the occasional slap.

It goes on for a time; Kestrel has no idea how long. She is too caught up by the pure sensation of it. She is a weeping, aching, shaking creature on the edge of all existence. Her body begs for more even though it longs for it to stop. Her breasts have begun to throb as the flogging becomes more intense and her teeth grit painfully as she tries not to use her safe word. It is too early and she wants this, but this is always the hardest part, going under into subspace, escaping to a place where the pain becomes so muted yet so beautiful. So good.

A second orgasm begins to rail through her. Her head snaps back on her neck and she howls at the ceiling, gobbling out what might be words; she begs for permission to cum and hears her mistresses laughing. Sweat pours from her and drool slides down her chin. She cannot find the control she needs to keep from cumming and they know it. They drive her relentlessly to her orgasm.

The second is even fierier than the first. The first was an almost involuntary reaction to the moment, a soulless reflex of muscles and skin, but this... she is carried up and away, feeling herself as she breaks free of the bindings and pain and flies somewhere else as she is carried along by waves of pleasure that come from the rhythmic slap and slash of the clever tails and the mocking teeth and nails of Mistress Winter.

Her bare shaven sex is bitten and licked, causing her back to arch. She shoves her ass further out in an attempt to get more, to have it all, and then her hips buck wildly as she is given more of that cruel mouth. Her cum spills forth, hot, sticky, and white. She can smell the sweat in her armpits and feel the runner's ache in her calves and thighs. Her head spins and she screams again and again as her body, so long denied of the pain that creates so much ecstasy, is given to her by two well-skilled Dommes.

The moment hangs suspended, stretching like taffy at room temperature, and then it snaps and she is sobbing, begging and asking for a pause. That word brings everything to a halt.

The monitor stops at the edge of the scene. She is a true sadist in every sense of the word, and seeing the helpless and lovely sub dangling and gasping makes her heart race. Her duty is to make sure that the subs' wishes are respected; that the play, which is always dangerous, does not become unsafe; and that nobody is playing above their skill level. She either does not know or pretends not to know that the reason she acts as monitor more and more these days is because she was never attractive and as she has aged, she has become dried up and hag-like. Since she is a stone butch, that rarely bothers her, but it does sometimes make her angry that the subs rarely want her.

The monitor is a woman who can be trusted with the position because she is so rigid that the baby butch dykes call her "ramrod" behind her back, and not because of the impossibly stiff and long cock she likes to wear. They think she is a nosy, smart-mouthed know-it-all, and they pretend to like her so she will stop lecturing them and leave them alone.

The monitor stares at the firm body of the sub, thinking of the women she culls from the Craigslist ads these days. They are always older or overweight. They are rarely into the scene. Every once in a while, a fairly attractive sub will listen to her spiel and decide the extreme play she likes - fishhook piercings and heavy whipping - are attractive offers. She thinks how unfair it is that she grew into a player in the dens of Amsterdam. That she was the daughter of a naval judge stationed in Germany, and that she has ridiculous skills and strength to use them, but they are going to waste because BDSM, which is supposed to be about mental over the physical, has degenerated into a scene where you have to be good-looking and below 40 years old to be appreciated. She deliberately ignores the players even older than she is who seem to have no trouble finding prey or predators while she thinks these things.

The sub has ended the pause and the monitor moves on. In the scene, the two Dommes are smiling. The sub is tied to the wall. Her ass is perched on a high standing table that has been shoved against the wall and chained there to prevent it from moving. She is in a slightly reclined position facing outward, her legs pushed back and wide open. Her arms are outstretched and her mouth is taped up with duct tape. Her breathing is apparent behind it; the silvery gag moves in and out with each ragged breath. In her left hand, she holds a bell to use if things get out of hand and she needs to stop the scene.

Mistress Winter has bound her legs tightly. Her thighs and calves are cinched together and her ankles are bound by and attached to the table's thick legs by short lengths of the rope. Her long black hair has been pulled up and back so that the mistresses can watch every delightful wince and grimace on her pretty face.

It is a hard position. It requires Kestrel to really work her stomach muscles and to stay loose at the same time. It takes her total concentration to ignore the burning in her muscles. She whimpers when Mistress Summer prances close with a bucket filled with wooden clothespins. Kestrel eyes them with tears falling; they wet the tape and roll off the end of her nose and Mistress Winter laughs and begins to pinch and twist her nipples, causing shivers to break out along Kestrel's spine.

She screams behind the gag when the

clothespins come. Mistress Summer lines them up, pinning open Kestrel's soft labia, and Mistress Winter tucks the pins neatly into the rope so that they cannot fall off or down. Kestrel screams over and over and her eyes begin to flutter as the pain causes her pussy to once again be soaked and ready.

"Nice, isn't it? Nothing burns like clothespins," Mistress Winter says, and then Kestrel screams again as the woman lines up the enormous strap-on with Kestrel's wet center and drives herself into it.

There is being filled to the end of her ability. There are the clothespins and the wet smacking sounds as the cock slams home again and again. There is the feeling of being all the way open; her legs, her helpless pussy, and her arms all combine to make her feel vulnerable and widened. Kestrel knows there is more to come and she screams as Mistress Summer begins to rub the vibrator against the rock-hard nub of her clit, forcing her to beg and plead behind the tape.

As a small act of mercy, Mistress Summer climbs aboard the table and cradles Kestrel's head tightly with one arm. Her eyes are slit with pleasure and she grinds her latex clad ass against the tabletop as she watches the bound and begging sub trying to stop the orgasm she is forcing from her from coming.

Kestrel is helpless to prevent it and Mistress Summer watches as cum once again streaks from that puffy and lovely pussy. She lets her eyes rest on the softness of its folds and the deep rosiness of it. The sight of it turns her on and she thrusts deeper and harder, the base of the strap-on rubbing deliciously against her clit and causing her own orgasm to spiral up.

"Yeah, how do you like that, you little slut? You like getting fucked with this big cock, don't you? It feels so good inside that pussy, doesn't it?" Mistress Summer pants out and the words create an unimaginable inferno in Kestrel. Her eyes open wide and she strains forward, a last scream building behind the tape. When she is reduced to a shivering and limp mass, the scene pauses once again. She is given water and is freed; she walks on the floor for a few minutes to restore her circulation and to give all three of them time to regain that small calm that keeps players from going too far.

When the play resumes, it is with Kestrel tied face down to the table once more. This time she is standing, and her upper body is pushed far forward, exposing her tender mound to the air and the stinging single-loop flogger. The flogger is for serious subs: it is painful in the extreme and leaves marks that cannot be hidden and won't fade for a few days. Mistress Summer has her hands full keeping it from wrapping as she throws it over and over. For her, the sight of raising red welts on that formerly flawless skin, the sound of the moans coming from Kestrel's mouth, and the scent of sweat and heated blood give her the rush.

An anal hook has been inserted into Kestrel. It is a large heavy stainless-steel hook that has a five-inch-diameter ball on one end and a large loop akin to the eye of a sewing needle on the other. The ball is inside Kestrel's anus; it rubs and fills her delicate hole. If she moves while the flogger comes down, the weighty ball moves inside her ass. It is a terribly exciting predicament to be in—and a painful one.

The loop end of the hook has a lengthy rope threaded through it. The rope is tied to the blindfold that covers Kestrel's eyes. In the dark, there is only stress, fear, and the disconcerting knowledge that they could leave her just as she stood and let anyone who chose to come in and fuck her. That she has no way to prevent anything that is going to happen to her—that she has become as helpless as she will ever be in her life.

"Right here, bitch."

Mistress Winter is in front of her.

Kestrel can smell her arousal and the musky scent of her pussy, and she moans even as her face is shoved into it. She can feel the dental dam—feel the way it slides across her delicate flesh—and she gasps for air and struggles against her bonds. Her hands are tied under the table and she cannot move at all; there is zero room for maneuvering, and she squeals and sobs as she is forced to pleasure the mistress who uses her carelessly and cruelly.

"Lick it here, you stupid fucking bitch." Hands are shoved into her hair and her head is bent forward and back. The ball moves inside her and the single-tailed flogger comes down again. It all combines to create a free falling feeling that is as awesome as it is rare. Kestrel loses her entire being. There is nothing left physically. She is once more simply sensation, pain, want, and desire. She can taste sweat and sex and her body is on the verge of total collapse. She is reaching her limits and she knows it. She cries out again and again in protest and joy as she is forced to serve again and again until Mistress Winter cums in huge waves that break across Kestrel's face.

The endorphins and the nerves are still running high. Kestrel is riding a rush so huge it threatens to engulf her. The two Dommes know it and they back off slightly, allowing her room while keeping her desire levels high by slapping her face lightly, mocking her and spanking. Kestrel moans out a thank you and please with every blow, every word, and grinds herself against the table edge in a desperate bid for relief.

She is untied from the table and thrust to the floor. Just the act of being on her knees sends her back into spasms of need. She is bent far over, and Mistress Summer shoves the sheathed strap-on into her mouth. Kestrel struggles for air. She gasps and tries to open her mouth wider to get air into the corners, but the cock is too big—it takes up everything. Drool runs down her chin and that makes the mistress laugh. She slaps Kestrel again, grabs her hair tightly, and forces herself so deep into Kestrel's throat that her crinkly auburn pubic hair tickles the sub's nose.

"You want to get that good and wet, you fucking whore," Mistress Summer taunts. "You better get it all wet 'cause it is going in your ass, bitch."

"No!" Kestrel chokes out as the cock slides out, and her denial is cut off like her air as the enormous cock is shoved back in. Saliva runs in cool silver streams and pools and puddles down on Kestrel's flushed breasts. Her nipples stand up in taut peaks and she bobs her head as she is bidden, cringing and sobbing as the ball works its way deeper inside her ass. Mistress Winter holds the rope tied to the eyed end of the hook high, yanking and tugging on it whenever Kestrel seems to be in danger of falling from her knees and onto her face.

Mistress Summer is enthralled with the way the sub is handling the cock. She gags and begs around it; her chest rises and falls rapidly. Looking at her, it is easy to see how much she wants this—her whole being is centered on wanting a cock to be shoved into her and on wanting to be beaten, used, and treated like the dirty thing she knows herself to be.

"You are worthless unless you have a cock in you, aren't you?"

Kestrel moans out a yes. Her eyes roll back; she knows that she is on the edge and that if she slips over, she will be punished. Her ass stings and aches, and even as she begs for it to stop, she can't help arching her ass upward as Mistress Winter begins to spank it hard. She can feel the redness, the soreness, and the misery in her ass. The ball is heavy, very large, and round. Her cheeks sing and sting and her back is in agony from the strain of the position she has been forced into.

Mistress Summer knows there is no time; if she is to keep control of this little pain slut, she has to take control of her right now. She snatches the hook from Kestrel's ass; it comes free with a loud sucking pop. She is not feeling kind so she brutally shoves her way in, bullying the cock inside and smiling at the screams that fill the room.

"Oh no, please. No, no, no!" Kestrel screams and sobs but she does not safe out and her hips betray her; she bucks wildly underneath the Domme's onslaught.

"Don't you fucking move!" Mistress Summer snarls and Kestrel tries to say yes to her mistress, but her head is snatched forward and Mistress Winter is filling her mouth with her cock. The movement rocks her back and forth; she is their helpless victim and they use her viciously. They thrust and fuck, pounding into her mouth and tender asshole. They pull her hair and slap her abused ass until she begs.

"You cum right now, you useless little slut." Mistress Summer commands, and Kestrel's legs shake and her pussy jets out long streams of her cum. She is a slippery gooey mess, and she is the happiest she has ever been.

Mistress Summer watches the skin pucker and open around her cock. She knows she is about to cum, and one look at her co-top's rapt expression tells her she is not the only one, so she yells out, "That's right, you fucking whore. You make us cum right now or I will fucking make you sorry."

Kestrel puts every ounce of her energy into it. Her mouth opens wider, she gags and chokes, but she gets every inch of cock into her throat. She holds her ass perfectly still so that the Domme behind her can give it to her as hard as she needs to in order to get off. Her body is in overdrive and she is weeping without knowing she cries. The tears have soaked the blindfold until it smells like the distant sea. Everything is darkness and joy and the feeling of being necessary, of being in pain so total, forever banishes the numbness of her existence as a Goody-Two-Shoes foster parent and abandoned-for-better-territory wife.

Mistress Summer removes the harness and cock and positions herself so that her pussy is in front of Kestrel. Kestrel knows what is expected of her. Slowly she lowers her head and begins to lick and suck at the pussy that is being arched up toward her face. The labia are delicate and thin; they are of soft coral color, with a slightly salty but still sweet taste. Kestrel finds herself wet again as she does her best to please the woman who has given her so much pleasure. Her eyes close and she sighs as her hair is roughly pulled to one side by Mistress Winter.

She can see suddenly, and it is then that she realizes that there are literally dozens of people standing close by watching her being beaten and fucked. For some reason, that turns her on even more.

She has never been on display before and has never had people watching her fuck or being fucked, and the thrill that races into her belly blooms even hotter in her crotch. She begins to play to the crowd, taking her time and making happy little sounds as she licks the cunt spread out before her in long sensual licks.

Mistress Winter begins to moan, her eyes rolling back as she arches her ass high in the air, her heels digging into the rough floor below her.

"That is right. You lick my pussy good now," she croons and her fingers tangle into Kestrel's long hair and she holds her face closer to the slippery hole.

Kestrel uses her tongue, making it stiff so that she can thrust it deeply inside the heated slit. She licks the cum-slick walls and groans when even more fluid leaks down her chin and lips. She can feel the tiny quivers on the other woman's inner thighs; this means she is doing a good job and she works her head faster and harder, her jaw aching and her lips feeling sore as Mistress Winter begins to buck and thrust her hips at her even faster.

Cum pours out of the juicy pocket of flesh that Kestrel is lavishing attention on and a long sigh comes from the onlookers.

She is yanked from her place and left to one side; her knees pressed into the cold floor while Mistress Summer positions herself above the body of her friend and then slides her heavy cock inside her.

Kestrel stares in lustful wonder as the cock opens Mistress Winter's pussy even wider. The two women arch and plunge at each other, their long hair tangling and swirling, their fingers grasping each other's asses and teeth, and lips working on nipples and the round globes of flesh that surround those hard peaks.

"Come here." Mistress Winter says and Kestrel crawls over and sits on the woman's face. From that vantage point, she can see very clearly the cock going in and out of her pussy. The sight fascinates her; the way the flesh pulls and sucks at it turns her on in a way she cannot explain and does not want to try to. All she knows is that it excites her and that her clit is being sucked and licked, fingers are moving inside her, and there is a nearly unbearable friction growing by the second.

Mistress Summer is fucking Mistress Winter harder; her hips are moving faster and faster and Kestrel feels a moment of panic. If she does not cum before they do, they may not allow her to. She wants to cum badly, she needs it desperately, and so she begins to ride Winter's face, rocking her hips from side to side and grinding her clit against the open mouth below them. A hand smacks at her jiggling ass cheeks and Summer laughs, a trifle breathlessly, as she fucks Winter even harder.

It has become a race, and they all know it. The spectators are giggling and talking; from where she is sitting, Kestrel can see very clearly the man who takes his long and stocky penis out. He begins stroking his shaft and the woman next to him sinks to the ground in one graceful movement; he turns his hips just slightly and his cock becomes buried in her mouth. That sight, coupled with the sight of the cock in Winter's pussy, sends Kestrel over the edge.

She screams as she cums, her whole body shaking in wave after wave of pleasure. The fingers become more insistent inside her pussy. They thrust harder and faster and she can hear the woman below her gasping as her own pleasure begins to peak.

Mistress Summer begins to moan and pant; her tits bounce up and down as she strains to get a little faster, her muscles going rigid as she finds her own orgasm and brings Mistress Winter to one at the same time.

The spectators are in for it as well. The man whose cock is buried in the woman's mouth begins to grunt and thrust his dick faster and harder into her; she moans and sways, her fingers squirming on the hard nub of her clit as his hands drag her closer. He pulls out as he cums, and Kestrel can see the heavy spurts of thick white cum hitting the woman's chin and chest. His cum splashes onto her nipples and she lifts her tit up and licks that splatter off with a happy grin that makes the others standing around break into spontaneous applause and smiles of their own.

The scene crashes to an end and they all slump into each other, breathing deeply and unable to even speak. The room smells of expended energy and sex stink. The Dommes are exhausted and trembling; the sub is in need of aftercare. Winter and Summer wave away the onlookers and the three women all cuddle up together, whispering small endearments at each other, and then they begin to giggle and ask each other questions as the long haze of afterglow wraps around them.

For the next twenty minutes, they just lay there, talking the scene over and asking what was liked the most, what was disliked, and what would be done differently. They lend each other warmth and comfort, and slowly they come out of the headspace that allows them to give such pain and to take it. As the rawness of the moment wears off, they slowly return to the people that are outside of the dungeon.

They get up and begin the task of tidying things up; others will need to use the space and it is considered unsportsman-like not to clean the scene up. Afterwards, Kestrel walks through the dungeon slowly, supported by the now-solicitous Dommes. She has served well and this care is part of her reward. They help her into her dress, kiss her face, and wipe her last bit of tears away. In this moment, they love her.

As Kestrel opens the door to walk away from the dungeon, two baby butches come in talking. One says, "You can't be afraid to let a sub teach you something. I mean you are new to this, so you have to learn how to respect them if you want them to respect you. You cannot simply hurt a sub any way you want to, and you never leave them hanging mid-scene because you engaged in something you could not find the guts to see all the way through. That is wrong and they will let everyone know what you did. Believe me; you do not want to have a sub tell the whole scene you are a bad or inconsiderate top. I mean, you can't hurt them mentally or physically or emotionally like that. This is serious stuff we are dealing with and you being selfish and unkind for the hell of it will really hurt a sub."

"How can you hurt someone who wants to be hurt in a wrong way?" asks the other baby butch, and the first says, "Well, you can abuse them within a scene and keep going after they safe out. Usually a monitor or another player will put a stop to that though—and really fast. You can ignore their limits or your own and cause a lot of physical damage just by inexperience and eagerness and then...well then there is the mental stuff."

"How do you hurt someone mentally?" asks the baby butch. She is eager to learn and ready to play, and the older one smiles and keeps giving her a lesson.

"You give them promises you do not intend to keep. You can promise them things like love outside the dungeon and then deny it. You can screw with their minds so they think that they are yours and then drop them just to get a kick out of seeing them cry. Or, and this is a really bad thing, you can play mind games with a sub to the point that you not only dominate them but also own them and then you deny them the care and respect they deserve from you for being willing to submit to you on such a level. Never tell a sub you love them if you don't. It's like leaving them hanging from a bad length of ordinary rope. It is that bad, that dangerous, and that damaging."

"You got to watch out for subs you do that to," says the monitor and for once the experienced baby butch does not wish she would shut her flapping, know-it-all mouth. "They will take revenge on you. I mean it, too. A sub has a lot of ways to get even. You don't ever want to hurt one outside of the way they agree to hurting. It is wrong to begin with, and you will suffer the consequences for it."

Outside the door, Kestrel walks to her car slowly. The sky is smutty and dark, a lone bird calls from somewhere, and she smiles as she thinks of the new Domme being trained inside. "At least she is being taught by someone who cares about her responsibilities as a top," she thinks. Too many tops are just in it for the rush. As a sub, she can appreciate the hard training Dommes have to endure, and it is nice to know that there are tops out there that truly understand and appreciate her sacrifice in there on that cold concrete floor.

She drives away, and as she drives, her body throbs with pain. She will wear the bruises for days. Her vision has softened and her tension has released. She lights a cigarette and begins to sing along with the radio. She sings and smiles all the way home.

The End

3 LOVING THE DAUGHTER OF SIN

All was not quiet in Uruk. Pleasure was the usual order of the day, and it was being sought in the perfumed boudoirs and willing flesh available at every turn, but an atmosphere of uneasiness hung about the great city of courtesans. Many knew their Queen, the goddess Ishtar, was unhappy, but few would have understood her reasons.

Ishtar stood on a balcony overlooking the golden spires and marble temples of the city. Her face was a perfect oval, highlighted by eyes the color of violets and hair whose blackness had the same blue sheen found on raven's wings. Her lips, sensually thick and naturally crimson, were twisted into an expression of discontent. Her crimson robe billowed open in the scented breeze, revealing a body that was a study in hard angles and cool paleness.

The goddess sighed as she stared down at her city. She was bored and wanted more than just the usual amusements so easily found in her kingdoms. She was a goddess of war, and sex, and she wanted, craved, battle. A wry smile curled her lips as she thought of how boring eternity could be for those who actually had to live it out, unless they found some distraction for themselves.

Looking for something to provide that distraction, she trained her eyes onto her kingdom, searching out something worth having, and her gaze sharpened when she found what she sought.

Battle and sex is just what I need, she told herself. Hunger bloomed in her belly as she strode into her chamber, where she donned her armor and picked up her sword and shield. In the cold hallways of her palace, the walls were adorned with many carved figures of people engaged in carnal acts, and as she stormed past the carved murals, it writhed and moaned, but she ignored them, in no mood to be distracted by such simple magic.

What she wanted was to hunt, and to fuck.

Neoma picked up the scattered bills on the tiny and dimly lit stage. Her senses were so acute that even in the dark she could see the audience, could smell the sweat, despite the thick cloud of cigarette smoke and cheap cologne. She had an almost uncanny ability to scent out the desperate and the predatory, a trick that she often found necessary to her very survival in the clubs that were known as gentlemen's clubs but rarely ever saw a gentleman coming through the door.

As she wearily slumped into a chair in the dressing room, she admitted to herself that it was better than working the streets. As a young woman, she had walked alone on the corners and had often found herself a target of pimps and other women who wanted less competition on their strolls.

She cut that line of thinking off. The last thing she wanted was to remember what had happened the last time she had been attacked by a pimp. To keep her mind from wandering in that direction, she sorted her bills, refreshed the too thick eyeliner around her startling green eyes, and fluffed her mane of strawberry blonde hair.

She gave her body a coolly appraising look. Her tits were small and firm, her nipples a soft blur of pink. Her belly was concave, and the black strapless bra she put on made a stark contrast to the stack of her ribs. The black lace stockings clung to the long and slim lines of her legs and the black stilettos made her even taller, leaner, and meaner.

A strange sense of unease filled Neoma as she stood staring into the mirror. The hair on the back of her neck prickled, and she looked carefully around the dressing room, but there was nobody else there. The bright lights showed the squalor of a thousand nights spent catering to the pleasure seekers: cigarette smoke stained the ceilings and walls; sticky puddles of liquor stained the ratty carpet and countertops; cosmetics were jumbled together; and clothes, both street legal and club wear, lay about in tangled heaps. There was nothing unusual or frightening about any of it, yet, she was afraid, and if there was anything Neoma had learned, it was to trust her instincts.

She could not place what it was that had her so frightened, but something had triggered her instincts. She grabbed her clothes and dressed as quickly as possible then ducked out the back door of the club. The trash-strewn alley was deserted, but she kept her back against the wall of the club as she navigated, despite that fact. The bricks of the building radiated coolness and she blinked, trying to see into the brightly lit street beyond. She sniffed the air, but all she got was the same scents that always rode the air. The hair at the back of her nape still stood up though, and she hesitated, wondering if she would be safer in the shadows.

A shape swooped over her head, and she caught a glimpse of something that gave off a hard silver shine. She somehow understood on some primitive, cellular level that a sword was being aimed at her head long before the thought could make itself known. There was a loud clatter as the sword struck the brick of the building behind her and sparks shot up into the night.

Wings beat the humid air. She didn't waste time screaming, she simply ran on, hoping to get herself into the pool of moonlight at the mouth of the alley. She could feel her body gathering heat, preparing to change as her feet propelled her forward.

The first time she had changed, she had been horrified. The need to feed had left her shocked and disgusted, and she had fought her urges for years. She ate raw meat that she heated just enough to make it more palatable, stayed away from the moonlight, and wore silver when the moon was the fullest to prevent the change, but at that moment, she knew morphing into her were-self was the only hope she had for survival.

The thing trying to kill her was not human, of that she was certain. It looked like a woman, wore a shining armor and helmet, but rode a solid white horse that had a set of powerful wings, which it used to gain flight. There was no way that the woman was a human, and when the female were-tiger emerged from the moonlight, all of her thoughts had narrowed to a simple focus: self-preservation and hunger.

Neoma attacked without finesse. She was fast but still unskilled. She managed to catch Ishtar by surprise, but that surprise did not last long enough for her to sink a claw or fang into her flesh. Ishtar charged in, dealing out a hard blow to the side of Neoma's head that brought pain, followed by blackness.

"So you're awake."

Neoma struggled against the bondage but to no avail. The silver chains were connected to cuffs around her wrists and ankles. No matter how hard she tried, she could not squeeze her fingers together tightly enough to get past the metal. The cold metal of the cuffs was frightening, and beneath her nude body was a softness that was somehow as exciting and decadent as it was terrifying.

She fought the urge to scream as the blindfold was removed but she did bite. Her teeth closed on empty air however, and laughter made her wish she had never tried it.

Her eyes throbbed as they adjusted to

the brilliant daylight pouring through the diaphanous curtains. The curtains fluttered in a breeze that smelled of the incense that the temples burned constantly.

"The priests are torn between wanting to worship me and wanting to depose me."

Neoma blinked at the beautiful woman who stood beside the bed. Despite the situation, her pussy throbbed at the sight of the woman's nude body. To her amazement, she found herself wanting to reach out and touch the black hair that covered the woman's pussy, slide her fingers inside her, and see if she was as wet and willing as she wanted her to be.

"You want to touch me?"

The amusement in that voice sent chills along Neoma's spine. She focused intently, blanking all thought from her mind and long seconds went by in a stony silence.

"You have no idea of why you are here, do you?"

"You kidnapped me because you're too cheap to pay for sex."

Sarcasm laced Neoma's words, but fear made her feel weak and slightly ill. She wasn't certain what had happened because there was an alarming emptiness where that memory should have been and she bit at her bottom lip, forgetting that the woman could read her thoughts as she tried to recall those lost moments.

"You are here to serve me."

The words were implacable, but Neoma was a product of the streets and cribs; she had been told to serve before and had refused, and she saw no reason not to refuse again, especially since she was beginning to think that one of the customers or girls had drugged her drink.

"Go fuck yourself."

The chains parted at a flick of the slender fingers. Neoma could not speak for a moment, but when those fingers ran from the center of her breastbone up to the pulse in her throat, she became acutely aware that the woman was no hallucination. Goose pimples bloomed on her skin, her pussy gave a painful throb of longing and her face flared red as cruel laughter made it known that her thoughts were being read again.

"Tell me your name."

Tell me yours." Neoma retorted.

"I am Ishtar, I am your goddess, and your Queen."

Neoma leaped from the bed and ran towards the open windows, where she stopped in dumbfounded amazement as she wondered again if she was lost in some drug-induced hallucination. The sky above her was a gorgeous shade of cerulean and streaks of white clouds laced the big blue dome. The sun shone down on tall spires, reflecting off the gold and precious jewels that capped towers that rose to dizzying heights. The smells of spices and bitter incense were even more intense out there on the balcony, which was surrounded by highly carved metal. Even as she watched, one of the tiny women inside the design cupped her breasts, winked and let her hand slide dreamily down her belly.

"This can all be yours."

The words were breathed against the back of Neoma's neck, and an involuntary shiver ran along her spine. Her hands came up and covered her naked flesh in a gesture she would have thought herself incapable of; she had lost shame as an emotion when she was a child.

"I never saw anything come free," Neoma replied bitterly. "So I'm willing to bet there's a price for this too."

Ishtar felt a growing lust for the beautiful young woman, but her voice betrayed nothing as she said, "There is. But it is a simple one. You never knew your kind, you were put outside your pack, left to fend for yourself and to live or die as the fates would have it. Your kind abandoned you, they put you in exile, and now is your chance to repay them for that."

Neoma's thoughts spun wildly. She was not alone, there were others like her, but where? And why had they put her out into the world, why had they left her alone?

Confusion battled her rage, and when she spoke, her words were choked and thick, "What do you want?"

"You are the most beautiful of your kind I have ever seen. I want you to serve me, to agree to serve me. All animals love me, why not you? Think of how loved you will be here, and how much you will love serving me."

Derision canted Neoma's lips, "I don't serve anyone."

"That explains why you have never been accepted into any of the high-class brothels, and peddle yourself on the streets and in the clubs instead, doesn't it? Do you enjoy that small freedom so much then?"

Ishtar didn't miss the way Neoma flinched at the words. Nor did she disregard the look of wariness and cynicism imprinted upon the delicate features of her face.

Ishtar reached for Neoma's arm as the younger woman attempted to stomp past her. A current of electricity flowed between them. In the sky above, the sun began to sink in a ball of fiery orange and red.

"Don't touch me." Neoma snarled.

"How dare you order me?"

Neoma's hands tangled into Ishtar's inky hair. She yanked the Queen's head backwards and the sight of the milky white arch of throat filled her with a hunger like none she had ever known.

Ishtar yelled in a mixture of pleasure and pain as sharp teeth nipped at her throat, and then it was Neoma who cried out, in the same mingling of sensations, as the goddess ground her hips against hers and turned her wet hungry mouth loose on her tender lips.

Neoma could feel every curve of Ishtar's body. The flesh covering the dangerous angles was incredibly soft and under it laid muscle. A groan spilled from her mouth as she was shoved back into the room.

Ishtar laughed as Neoma fell onto her knees, unconsciously assuming the position that pleased her most.

"You are going to serve me well."

The words rang in Neoma's ears. Rage and lust met pain as she was dragged across the room by her hair. Her knees scraped the floor and a howl broke from her throat, but she found herself unable to escape from the cruel grip.

Ishtar was so caught up in her own desire that she ignored the moonlight that filtered through the transparent draperies. The pewter shine drifted across the floor, and then it touched Neoma's flesh.

Ishtar found herself grasping the rough pelt of a furious were-tiger, and she wisely let go and backed away. Her eyes darted around the room, seeking a weapon, and a grin crossed her lips as she spotted the silver chains.

Neoma leaped at Ishtar, and the two rolled across the tile. A growl of fury came from the starved were-tiger, and Ishtar laughed as adrenaline shot through her. A challenge was something she saw too rarely, and she bit and clawed with abandon as she rolled her body over the body of the were-tiger, and her laughter was even more delighted when she was pinned to the floor by the beast.

The battle raged for long minutes. Neoma was young and strong, but Ishtar was as wily as her Valkyrie and used to war. She led Neoma in the direction of the bed, watching the magnificent tiger with the strawberry colored fur stalk her and feeling the heated pulse in her crotch.

Ishtar jumped onto the bed and Neoma pounced as Ishtar knew she would. Before the were-tiger could bite, she was neatly cuffed and trussed, and her human form reasserted itself.

Neoma screamed with rage, and her fists beat into the mattress, but not for long. She was hauled upright, the bed giving under her feet and the chains rattling madly as Ishtar loosed them from the frame but not from her body.

She tried to run but Ishtar grabbed her by her hair. Her feet pedaled in a puppet-like dance at the abrupt halt to her flight, and then she was screaming again as the chains were hoisted high over her head and fastened there.

A slow deliberate breath at the back of her neck hushed her. A quiver of pure desire ran over her body as her hips were dragged backwards; her ass forced to arch up higher while her back curved into a C shape.

The skin stretched over the taut flare of her ribcage broke out in goose pimples as hands, deceptively soft, slid across it. Fingers gently caressed her tender nipples, and Neoma's eyes went wide as they turned cruel and twisted that flesh into hard and eager peaks.

Teeth nipped at her neck and trickles of fluid ran down her thighs. Ashamed, Neoma tried to force her legs together, to stop the sensations exploding inside her. A hard slap on her ass bolted her eyes open again.

Pain and fear met anger, but all she could do was twist and growl in her bondage. Her pussy wept more juice as Ishtar forced the smooth muscle of her thigh between Neoma's open legs and ground it against the wet mat of strawberry-blonde curls that lay there.

Neoma shuddered and whimpered. She told herself she could not, did not, want what the Queen was giving to her, but to her shame, she found herself rocking her hips against the movement of that thigh. She forced herself to look down, and tears fell from her eyes as she saw the glistening streaks that proved that her unwillingness was a lie.

"Say you yield and I will let you come." Ishtar snarled and Neoma shook her head, unable to say the words.

Ishtar withdrew her thigh and Neoma cried out. Her pussy throbbed with want and need, her arms ached from the bondage, and she jerked forward reflexively when Ishtar moved once more behind her.

The slap was light, almost contemplative. Then nails raked lightly down Neoma's ass cheeks. Fingers slid across them, dipped into the cleft between them and were gone too quickly. She whimpered over and over as the slaps grew harder, as the fingers began to probe deeper and stay longer and the time between each onslaught grew less.

"You like that, don't you?"

There was a taunting note in Ishtar's voice that made Neoma tighten her resolve, but it crumbled as fingers slid around her body and tweaked her nipples then dove lower to the soft nest of her pussy hair.

"Fuck you!" She yelled as demanding fingers rubbed her clit.

The tangible world slid away with every stroke and blow. Neoma became a creature of sensation as Ishtar carefully sensitized her skin with scratches, bites and slaps and then gave her pleasure as a reward. Her muscles and nerves jumped; her mind translated the pain of Ishtar's teeth on her neck into pleasure, and when Ishtar stepped back and began the spanking again, she willingly arched backwards, giving herself over to it.

Neoma hung there, caught in an apex of lust and agony, while Ishtar refused to allow her the final moment. It was a battle and they both knew it, but with every passing second, she became more and more certain that it would not be she that would win it.

Breath slid across the delicate flesh at the top of her ass cheeks. Neoma stiffened and then she screamed as teeth, both savage and undeniable, tore into that delicate flesh. She tried to run, but Ishtar's hands shot out and grabbed her hips, holding her hostage as she put her brand on that skin.

Sobs broke from her and she kicked backwards, but Ishtar was gone. She tried to twist around to see the woman, but before she could, Ishtar appeared again in front of her.

Ishtar sank to her knees, and the sight of the Queen in so humble a position stunned Neoma, leaving her unprepared when the raven-haired beauty leaned forward and placed her mouth on her pussy.

Exquisite pleasure rippled upwards from her cunt to her belly as a warm mouth and tongue suckled and licked at her. Neoma could not do anything to guard herself against such delight. Her hips arched upwards, and her mouth opened in a moan of surrender as her clit was nipped at and then stroked with a knowing caress.

Ishtar worked her tongue under Neoma's hood, eagerly licking away the fat drops of creamy white come, reveling in the sugary-salty taste of her pussy. To add to her captive's torment, she slid two fingers along the seam of her pussy, before sliding them inside. Neoma's walls tightened on her fingers, and a hot burst of liquid dripped down her hand.

"You are going to come." Ishtar said into the wet heat of Neoma's cunt. "Am I not a good Mistress then? Do you not adore me?"

"No!" Neoma yelled, in protest against Ishtar's words and the orgasm she could not stop.

Come spurted from her in thick white pulses. Ishtar did not let up; she kept her mouth and fingers working against that flesh until she had gotten every drop of what she wanted from the young queen of the were-tigers. When there was nothing left, Neoma hung in her chains sobbing, and cursing Ishtar and herself, the older Queen stood.

Neoma gave her a baleful glare, but to her surprise, Ishtar bestowed upon her a tender kiss. It brought the taste of her own pleasure to her lips and she shivered in remembered bliss and hatred.

"You choose," Ishtar whispered into her captive's ear. "Stay or go, it is up to you. Stay here and you will serve me, or leave and be free, the choice is yours."

"I will fight you every step of the way."

"That is why I chose you."

The chains rattled as Neoma was freed from their grasp. She stood there, panting and sore, but far from broken.

"You may hunt," Ishtar said as she pointed toward the doors that led to the balcony. "You have my permission to be your wild self, but you must return here if you want to be mine. That is my condition, do you accept it?"

Neoma paused on the brink of change and a happy smile lit her face, "I will serve you willingly. Come and get me when you want me."

The were-tiger leaped from balcony to balcony, growling and intent on feeding. Its nose turned upward to sniff the air, seeking blood, and above her, a goddess stood, looking down with lust kindling in her belly at the thought of the next night's hunt.

Neoma felt a breath on the back of her neck, and she whirled around, her senses going keen, but there was nobody to be seen. The feeling of being watched, of being stalked, did not abate however.

Neoma turned back to the dressing table, it was a far cry from the rooms of the clubs, but it was still just a room where she was expected to dress and to groom herself until she was an approximation of every man's fantasy. Or at least, the men who came to the expensive and exclusive theatre of which she had become a cast member.

Red roses dripped fragrance into the air, lilies sent their scent from the candles, and she shuddered slightly as a cool breeze rippled across her nipples, stroking them into firm high peaks. Her eyes closed in pleasure as she felt fingernails scratching along her back and the tender flesh of her ass cheeks. Then the sensation vanished, and she was left alone and with a strange sense of vulnerability riding her senses.

The mirror showed her body: long, lean, and very pale. Her hair fluffed out around her face and her makeup was perfect; she had drawn catty corners onto the ends of her eyes, elongating them, and then she had applied green glitter to her lids as well as feathery long eyelashes. The result was undeniably sexy and mysterious as well as whorish.

She stroked her fingers along her sides, reveling in the satiny texture of her own skin. The narrowness of her waist, and the swell of her hips pleased her; she ran a finger inside the red-gold curls that covered her lips, stroking lightly before parting those puffy and fluid-slicked lips.

Her finger stroked her clit, and there was an unmistakable sound from beside her. It was a gasp, and she not only heard it, she felt the puff of air from it as well, hot breath gusted across her skin momentarily before it vanished.

Neoma spun around once more, her eyes widening and her nostrils flaring as she tried to discern from where the breath had come. She sniffed the air and then she sprang forward; for one second, her body came in contact with someone else's flesh; she could feel hard muscle and soft curves, but then it was gone and she landed sprawling on the thick carpet.

Knock sounded on the door, "Neoma, you have two minutes!"

She gritted her teeth and forced herself to call out pleasantly, "I will be right there!"

Again, her senses on full alert, she tried to find the presence in the room, but to no avail. A small hint of musky perfume and incense hit her nose, and a wicked grin curled her lips. She slid her costume on, ignoring the frantic pounding on her door; the outraged stagehand who hated for the performers to be late could not phase her at that moment, and when she strutted out of the room, she knew that whatever it was that was in her room, it would be there when she returned as well.

Out on the stage, the lights pulsed pink and scarlet. Streaks of gray and silver shot through those brilliant pulses, and she took her place center stage. She held her head high, and the two fans in her hands were fluttering in the breeze made by her fingers by lightly lowering and lifting from their surfaces.

The art of burlesque had been lost on Uruk at one time, but thanks to the restless citizen who had imported several earth women as slave girls, it had made a comeback. Neoma had stumbled into the theatre one evening and watched the women working their magic, and she had been enthralled by it to the point that she had gone home to her tiny crib and begun to practice fiercely the soft and sensual movements and the rhythms of it.

She bumped her hips, pulled off one

long silver glove with her teeth, spun it around her head, and then used it to spank herself on one lean hip. The men at the theatre were not like the men at the clubs, they did not lean forward, their greedy eyes straining at the sockets to watch her. Their hands did not cup their fingerprint-smeared glasses desperately. On the whole, they seemed rather amused by the whole dance, and she knew that that was not the case at all, they were simply more used to paying for what they wanted and they could afford it as well.

The men who frequented the theatre held the ears of the rich, the political, and the ones who lived in the castles that rode the clouds at the very horizon's edge. At that thought, Neoma remembered the feel of silver chains around her ankles and wrists, and a throb of lust hit her hard, making her pussy quiver with longing.

A small trickle of fluid leaked out and slid down her inner thigh. The lights shone off of that tiny trail, and the men lost their facades of composure, leaning forward and letting small sighs escape their mouths. Almost immediately they recovered, but here and there, she saw the unmistakable eye shine of wolves and vampires. That made her smile harder. Her own eyes were covered by the glitter and the eyelashes, none of them would be able to see through the simple and sparkling disguise to her real true eyes below.

Her set ended, and she walked amongst the crowd. The theatre did not offer lap dances or private rooms; instead cool little bowers filled with fresh flowers and champagne sat at small intervals and a man, or woman, could sit there beside the dancer of his choice and make very discreet arrangements with the manager of the club as to what they wanted and when and how much the evening would cost them.

Neoma had many repeat clients. A few never made it back to the theater however, and she was very, very careful to make sure that the ones that she chose to feed from were those that staggered in, suddenly flushed with money from some high stakes game or another. Nobody missed them, their kind ran across Uruk like parasites, and one more dead gambler or hustler hardly mattered.

She would have loved to eat a few of the men she had as regulars, she was fairly certain that things would improve with their removal from power, but she left them whole and sound when she left their beds, despite her wishes to the contrary.

There was a small breath across her cheek as she entered the dressing room, and she spun sideways; that time, her teeth were already bared and her claws were out. Blood sparkled in the air; small drops of it landed on the carpet and sizzled there.

The smell of it, coppery and rich, filled Neoma's nostrils. Hunger exploded in her chest, but just then, a figure materialized and a hunger of a different kind entirely filled her belly.

"Hello little darling," Ishtar said silkily right before her lips came down on Neoma's.

The kiss was fierce and vicious. Ishtar's lips demanded that Neoma open her own, and she did. Their tongues met and twisted, and their hands began to run up and down each other's skin hungrily.

"You missed me, say it." Ishtar demanded, but Neoma broke off the kiss and shoved the goddess away.

Ishtar watched her prey walk away with amused eyes. She could read the were-tiger's thoughts; she wanted to fuck and be fucked. She wanted to have her pussy spread wide and her nipples sucked hard and well. The men and women who paid her for sex never touched her where it really mattered; to them, her sexual needs were nil, and it was theirs that were paramount. Neoma understood that, and did not really care, but unsatisfying sex often left her starved for sex that would make her wet, make her beg, make her come until she went limp.

Ishtar knew that as well and was determined to give that to her, and to give it to her very hard.

The air crackled with tension and energy. The high windows that overlooked the boulevard billowed open suddenly, and the smell of the night came inside, effectively ridding the room of its too heavy perfume and the languor that the incense and fragrances of it caused.

Ishtar knew that that was the true purpose of the rich furnishings, the flowers, the foods arranged temptingly on the platter that sat on the long silver side table. The owners of the theatre deliberately stunned their women with those things, hiding spells in the comforts. She had been watching from her castle as Neoma pleasured the theatre's customers, and while she did not care about too many of her citizens, she had begun to feel a fierce jealousy every single time she watched Neoma slide across a bed that had someone other than herself in it.

The time had come for her to make Neoma her own. The problem was that she wanted the wildness of the were-tiger and the independence of the woman to remain unbroken. The puzzle had proven to be nearly insolvable, until earlier that morning.

"Here kitty, kitty," Ishtar taunted, and then she jumped from the window.

Neoma did not pause. Her feet took her across the room and she plunged down; the walls of the theatre raced by and she landed on her feet silently, a gorgeous creature with red-gold fur and a set of emerald green eyes. Her long body was rife with muscle, and she ran toward the scent of the goddess, heading for the puddles of moonlight that congregated at the base of the building opposite the theatre.

There was a heavy crash from somewhere, and the smell of smoke. Momentarily confused, she looked around, an instinctive fear of fire filling her. Red yellow flames danced at the top of the theatre's roof, and when she looked toward the moonlight again, she saw Ishtar mounting her winged horse, preparing for flight. Neoma growled and ran after her, her muscles bunching and jumping under her pelt.

Just as she gathered herself to jump, Ishtar called out a spell and it was the women, not the were-tiger that slid to a crashing halt at the base of the building.

"Choose," Ishtar said, and her voice held no room for argument. "Wear my collar, agree to be mine and ride with me, or stay here on these dirty damn streets, go back to your life."

"You burned down the theatre," Neoma pointed out.

"It was a place of evil spells."

"Why don't you care more?"

"I need a reason to love." Ishtar said softly. "Will you be that reason?"

She held out her long slim hand and Neoma took it. She slid her leg over the back of the horse, and its mighty wings beat at the air and then they were soaring up and away and toward the castle.

Neoma had known that Ishtar would return for her sooner or later. The time had been the hardest thing to bear. As a were-tiger, she was immortal, for her time had so little meaning. She knew Ishtar was also immortal; they could spend three hours in their own world only to find a year had passed in mortal time. She had not realized how bound to the theatre she had been until Ishtar had broken the spell, and she found herself wondering just how long she had been there, a century, a week? Did it matter really?

Ishtar wasted no time when they reached her bedchamber; she hustled Neoma inside, slammed the door and ordered her to strip naked.

Neoma laughed and then she sauntered over to the balcony. The moonlight touched her body, casting the curves of her ass into relief and turning the column of her spine into a long series of delicate knobs as frail and fabulous as a classical sculpture.

Ishtar knew what she needed. She stalked toward her and grabbed her, her fingers tangling deeply into the hair at the base of Neoma's scalp. Her mouth came down, and once more, she plundered Neoma's sweet lips with her own. The kiss was so fierce that Neoma could feel her lips growing puffy and bruised from it.

Her heart began to beat high and fast, her breath came in a long gasp, and she splayed her fingers out in a gesture that said it all as Ishtar dragged her to the bed and tossed her across it.

"I am not going to chain you today darling," Ishtar said softly as she opened a drawer and pulled out a large cock and a leather harness with which to hold it in place. "But you are going to anyway, aren't you?"

Neoma could only nod as Ishtar fell onto the bed and then her mouth reached Neoma's tight pink nipples. Her teeth nipped and grazed at them, her hands stroked and kneaded the white flesh around those nipples, taking as much as she could while her knees nudged Neoma's legs apart.

Sensations exploded inside Neoma; her mouth opened in a soft cry as a hand stroked lovingly at her center, parting her nether lips and spreading the growing moisture there across the labia.

Ishtar ducked down, her face positioned above the strip of damp red-gold curls, and her lips began to tease her captive. She flicked her tongue out, barely allowing contact between its pointed tip and the fluid-slicked lips below it.

Neoma jumped and shivered at the teasing caresses and her fingers dug into Ishtar's ebony curls as she tried to arch her hips upward. She knew she had agreed not to move, she had not expected her to have placed a spell on her to make her utterly unable to do so. She should have known though, she thought wryly as Ishtar began sliding a single finger inside her.

Friction built up inside her as a second finger was added, then a third. Whimpers broke from her throat and her eyes closed as she felt the first stirrings of an orgasm.

Ishtar pulled back; she could smell the arousal on the flesh that she was sucking and teasing, and she wanted it to slow down. She raked her nails down Neoma's thighs, leaving stinging trails of pain and lust on that smooth skin, and then she bent her head to her pussy again. Her tongue found the hardened nub of her clit, and she began to stroke it, licking and sucking then moving away when Neoma's muscles began to grow rigid and her breathing became shallow. Every single time Neoma hovered on the very edge of an orgasm, Ishtar would pull away and leave her there, begging and pleading for release.

"Please," Neoma finally cried as her pussy ached and throbbed with need; she could feel how swollen and hard her clit was, and the fluids coming from her had literally soaked the bed below her ass. "Please just let me come, I will be good, I promise."

"Maybe I do not want you to be good," Ishtar replied, but she moved upwards anyway.

Neoma moaned as long hard inches filled her wet hole. She could feel herself stretching open to accept that thick length and she knew that Ishtar was deliberately giving her as much as she could handle. She was testing her out to see how far she could stretch, how much she could take.

Ishtar went slowly into the wet flesh that parted for her, at first. Once inside, she pulled almost all the way out, watching the shaft being caressed by the pink lips through which it entered as she plunged back inside Neoma.

"Fuck me back," Ishtar said as her hands slid under Neoma's ass and cupped it.

Immediately, Neoma felt her ass moving in time to Ishtar's pumping hips. Her pussy felt wide open and pleasantly full, her legs wrapped around Ishtar's narrow waist, and her fingers tangled into the black hair as their mouths met in a fierce kiss.

The scent of sex was very strong. Neoma inhaled it and her fingers trailed down Ishtar's smooth back, sliding in and out of the cleft of her ass, running along the clenching globes of her ass.

"I want you to come," Ishtar said. "So you will, and you will do it right now."

Neoma did. Her pussy contracted and expanded, her breath became a hoarse pant, and her fingers left huge slashes on her lover's skin as her nails went deep in the flesh that she tried to hold onto as her ecstasy overwhelmed her.

Ishtar pulled the cock out of her hole, enjoying the sight of the glistening fluids along its length. She grabbed Neoma by the hair and pulled her up to a kneeling position at the side of the bed, and then she herself slid off and stood on front of the beautiful woman she had captured.

"Open your mouth," she ordered, feeling pleased when Neoma did so without protest.

The cock went deeply into Neoma's throat. The taste of her own pussy filled her mouth, and she felt desire spurt hotly in her belly and more juice spilled down her legs as Ishtar spoke in a voice made her thick with lust.

"Suck it all clean my good little girl, drink every drop of your come off of my cock."

Neoma did, her mouth opened wider and her head bobbed faster. Ishtar tangled her fingers into Neoma's hair, her nails digging at her scalp as she pumped her hips harder and faster, her own eyes closing as her orgasm swept through her. Cunt juice leaked into the leather of the harness and lay in creamy white drops in her black pubic hair. She backed away and removed the harness, then spread her legs and thrust her pussy into Neoma's face in a command that she did not have to utter.

Neoma's tongue went to work cleaning every rich drop from the labia, spreading them out wide, and then her tongue slid upward to the clit, and then she hardened it and went inside the folds, enjoying every second of the decadent taste and pleasure of it all.

They lay together for a short time, their bodies cooling, and then Ishtar got up and walked to a chest that sat at the far end of the room.

"I had this made for you," she said as she came back to the bed.

Neoma stared at the slender silver collar that dangled from Ishtar's fingers. Her thoughts felt chaotic and jumbled, and her body felt bruised and sore, but yet she still wanted more. She still felt like if she did not get a few more moments of Ishtar's hands, tongue, and cock, she would simply die.

"If you take this, it means you are mine. That does not mean that you will never be allowed to be the wild creature that you are, you can remove it to hunt. You have the choice. Stay with me and swear your loyalty or leave here forever, what is it going to be?"

Neoma closed her eyes and thought about all the nights that she had laid under clients, and thought of the magnificent tortures that Ishtar had shown her. She allowed the aching throb in her pussy to filter into her thoughts and then she looked at the woman standing before her holding a silver collar.

"I accept," she said simply. "I am yours, always and forever."

Ishtar could not hide the grin that crossed her lips. She placed the collar around the slim column of Neoma's throat and stepped back.

"You better run," she said casually. "If I catch you, I am going to fuck you in that sweet and tight little ass."

Neoma jumped from the bed and her teeth gleamed as she laughed. The hallways were cool below her feet, and her heart pumped blood into her veins. Behind her, she could hear Ishtar laughing.

Love is funny, she thought happily, as she raced down an empty corridor, and how much fun we are going to have throughout eternity.

4 A GOOD READ INDEED

Jenna stared out at the lake, wondering if anyone could read the guilt on her face, she doubted it but she still wondered. Her knees were pressed together, her mouth hung open a bit, and there was still a bit of telltale flush on her cheeks from the powerful orgasm that had just swept through her.

Her panties were undeniably sticky and she could smell her pussy on her fingers when she raised her hand to push the hair back from her face. That scent caught her by surprise, but so had the sudden and almost blinding need to masturbate.

The reason for the surge of desire lay face down in the grass and she stared at it, both fascinated and repulsed, wondering how she could have ever been turned on by the thing in the first place.

But she already knew that answer. The book had a cover that featured a woman on her knees in a dirty alley with her face pressed into the crotch of a person in leather pants. She had guessed the other person was a woman by the shape of the hips but it was impossible to tell, as there were only those pants, those pants that were as sexy and slick as oil on a midnight river.

The book's pages riffled in the small breeze blowing in off of the quiet lake and she found herself looking down toward the house where the usually noisy Miller clan took their summer vacations. With Labor Day weekend three days gone, the lake was mostly deserted and silent, all the boats were safely inside, the kayaks and canoes were turned upside down and taped over. The large houses that were the residences of the summer crowd were mostly shuttered and dark, only the small houses where the locals lived showed light in the windows when dark finally fell.

Jenna didn't mind. She had purposely stayed late at the lake, she had no reason to go back to her apartment in the city just yet and she had been looking forward to some much needed quiet and solitude. But she had not had much peace at all because she had found the damn book shoved down in an old box she had bought from a garage sale and she had been anything but restful ever since.

She peeled the wrapper off of her sandwich and bit deeply into sprouted grain bread and rich goat's cheese. The very act of eating made her remember the story she had just read, the story that had caused her to have to lie down on her side in what she had hoped looked like a good facsimile of sleepy sunbathing while she rubbed her clit fiercely with her fingers.

She had to grin at that, she was wearing a loose sundress and sandals and while it was not exactly sunbathing attire it was close enough.

She sighed and picked the book back up, and re-read that story that had made her need to come so badly she had been willing to risk being seen by anyone still on the lake.

BLUEBERRIES

The table looks like it is set for someone's idea of an old fashioned and romantic summer dinner or maybe high tea. You know what I mean; long white linen tablecloth hanging just the perfect amount of inches from the green, green grass, a centerpiece of roses and lilies in a sweet pink vase that match the tiny flowers embroidered onto the edges of the napkins. That soft pink is further echoed by hand painted twins to those flowers that reside on the ceramic napkin rings.

There is the hum of a drowsy bee from somewhere and the flatware flashes its high sparkle at the sky, trying to outdo the sun. The serving platters are sterling silver with matching domes standing tall, the dishes are made from china so wafer thin it is nearly transparent. The very best in other words. The glasses are crystal, the water inside them bottled and home to the slices of lemon that float placidly over small ice floes. She is sitting in one of the white painted chairs, her body turned sideways so that she is facing away from the table and towards me. A piece of pie resides on a small saucer she holds in one long and elegant hand. The crust is tender, flaky and when cut it does not shatter, it gives way to the fork easily and splits to reveal plump and perfect blueberries.

"Come here," she says in her husky voice and I go to her on my knees in the fragrant grass, feeling it tickling my sensitive and naked skin, its scent creeping into my nose. She places one, just one, berry on her foot, right in the spot where her toes and foot meet. I wait, and she chuckles, she had thought to fool me, "Have it sweetie," she says and I nip it between my teeth like a puppy would, gently and softly.

The berry bursts in my mouth. It tastes of sunshine and far away fields. It tastes of sweetness and my hunger ignites, flames up my very spine but I say nothing. She would send me away from her table if I dared. A second berry is laid down for me. This one is set on the highest part of her foot, next to the spot where it joins that long slender leg and I take it with a small sigh of happiness. She knows I am pleased to be there at her feet and she pats my head affectionately to show me that she approves of my behavior and manners.

"Good girl," she murmurs and then she places a sugar and fruit soaked sliver of crust on her kneecap. I have to raise up to get it and before I do I whimper a little in my throat to seek her permission to do so.

"Come on sweetie," she says and I feel another strong surge of lust as I place my mouth above that polished and glowing skin, the bone so close to that surface and her body smelling of such wonderful things that I almost burst into tears when I just touch my lip to that skin. The softest touch is what is, a feather brushing lightly, a moment passing by unnoticed. The crust melts in my mouth like a sacrament,

Holy, holy I think...lines from an old poem coming back to me.

The small morsel is gone too fast and I whine without meaning to, which earns me a not hard but certainly warning little slap on my naked ass to remind me what I am. I understand it immediately and subside while she waits to see if I will control myself. When she is satisfied that I will she places a smaller sliver, smaller because I disobeyed, on her other kneecap and I take it, slowly relishing the taste, trying to make it last but it dissolves and fades anyway.

Inch by inch the trail creeps upwards. I touch my reverent lips to her outer thighs, her inner thighs, her upper thighs. I follow the trail to the part of her she really wants to feed me. Finally, she is ready for me to eat; she spreads her legs wide and slides to the end of the chair. A pink the same hue as the others in her table's color scheme peeks out at me from beneath blond curls.

"Lick me here," she says and her fingers with their long and pointed pastel pink nails open that juicy pocket of flesh, reveals the tender morsel she keeps hidden and I put my tongue out and taste of it gratefully.

Her hands hold me in place as she bucks her hips into me. I whine softly as she arches higher, harder, faster. She tells me to look up, to look at her and I do. I keep my eyes trained on her perfect face as she grunts and grinds her pussy into my mouth and all of its flavors come into me, run down my throat and chin. The taste of her is sweet and slightly salty. Her cum is oil that is heavy and white but oh so clean and I swallow obediently as she feeds it to me, her own eyes closing in a minute's long orgasm.

She is not yet finished though, the silver platters on the table are not empty and so she pushes me away unkindly in order to open one and I want to look, to see what is on it but I do not move. I wait patiently as she laughs and then hums a small snatch of melody I have never heard before. The platter held her harness and she waves it in front of my face, taps me on the nose with the cock and laughs at the expression on my face.

"Are you my good girl?" She asks while she straps on and I make a low happy noise in my throat and stick my tongue out in a happy panting agreement. "Since you opened it," she says. Before I can understand my mistake, she has captured me and the cock is in my throat. It is deep and hard in there. It is a choking and unkind thing and I thrash about, churning up the dirt under my knees but only momentarily because she laughs again and slows down, her hands on either side of my face and her hips moving almost dreamily as she fucks my mouth.

I whine and whimper but I can feel the hot fluid leaking down my own thighs. I am so lust stricken I want to scream, beg, and ask for it. I want to swallow all of her and she knows it, she whispers I am good, a good girl indeed and gives it to me. She feeds me her cock like she fed me the pie and her pussy. She feeds me and I wriggle my ass in the air and whimper as I look up at her, knowing she likes to see that hard cock sliding wetly from my mouth, likes to see my puppy dog eyes fixed on hers in a look of longing and pleading.

I am awash with desire. My nipples are hard and tight, my clit aches and throbs. I want to hump the grass, her leg, anything at all. The late afternoon air flows around my ass, drifts across my wet pussy, makes me lose my breath and whimper louder yet. I want it and she fucking knows it.

"I think you deserve a treat," she says and I have to force myself not to say anything as she pulls out of my throat. She waits to see if I will and when I don't she pats my head again; I love it when she acknowledges me as a good girl. I close my eyes and nudge her hand as she pats and strokes the top of my head, bumping my nose into her leg and licking her thigh once and only once because that is all she will allow me even when she is happy with me.

The bowl is wide and low. The ice cream is rich and homemade, straight from her churn and kept cold on a tray that has been lined with small chunks of dry ice so that it would not melt and ruin her dessert, her reward to me. I am so excited I want to leap about and nose her out of the way of my bowl but good manners were the first and harshest lessons she ever taught me so I wait patiently for her to place the bowl on the seat of the chair in which she was sitting not so long ago.

She watches me as I eat. She likes to see me licking at the heavy cream that she has filled with the same ripe blueberries that she baked into the pie. They swirl into the ice cream, leaving almost purple streaks in the delicious frosty treat that has been made with fresh ingredients from an old recipe.

I shiver as she positions herself behind me and then she is inside me, pulling my right leg up higher and propping it up on the small footstool so she can get to my clit more easily with the long and powerful vibrator. I am all sensation now; ice cream in my mouth, her cock inside me, and my clit throbbing against the purring thrum of the vibrator. I make a low primitive growl in my throat and she laughs and strokes harder until she is slamming into me and making my ice cream slop out of the bowl as my face splashes into it.

I want to come. I want to come and I have to balance myself so carefully on the balled up fists inside the tight mitts that remind me not to use my hands and I am weeping but still licking and lapping at my treat because she is watching me over my own shoulder and she will not be pleased if I do not lick that bowl clean. And besides, I want to come and I want to eat the food she made just for me.

Blueberries, ahhhhh the sweetness of the last of the summer's best fruit and the feeling of her inside me so big and hard, stretching me open, stretching me wide. I begin to whimper helplessly and I have to remember not to move, not to buck or fuck her back. My mouth is filled with blueberries and cream...oh...she is making me come and I am whining and shivering all over my body and then she says it, says the words I need to hear so desperately.

"Come to me, my pet," she says and in her voice is her own orgasm.

I growl as the total sexiness of it hits me, shakes me, rocks me and I come in a hard thudding gush on that enormous cock that she is pounding in and out of my soaked and slick pussy. We are outdoors, we are naked, we are fucking, we are eating and feeding and I am coming while she fucks me and she is coming while I let her fuck me.

When she is finished, she pulls out of me and I curl up in on the warm grass in a patch of sunlight that has gone the hard tarnished color of cheap promise rings that really mean nothing. I watch her with sleepy eyes as she begins the task of cleaning up and every once in a while she will stop in her labors to pat my head or scratch my chin, it is her way of showing me how loved I am by my owner.

"Come inside my sweet girl. I want to give you a bath and since you were so good today you get to sleep in the bed with me," she says in the voice she always uses when she is proud of me and pleased with me.

I practically die from excitement at that and she laughs while I romp and prance at her feet to show her how thrilled I am to be her good girl. She walks toward the house as I scamper along beside her and when she opens the door I tumble inside with a happy smile and rush down the hall to the open bathroom door where I wait for her, wait for my owner to come and bathe me.

I know what we have is not for everybody but it suits me to a T. I am a loved and well-fed pet. What more could I want? I have this and it is everything.

Jenna shivered again and began to gather up her things. She folded the red and white checked blanket and dropped it in her small hamper along with the wine bottle that was still half-full and the sticky balloon glass, the few small slivers of dark chocolate and the heavy macadamia nuts, the remains of her sandwich and a small bowl of fruit. She had read the story the night before and had begun to crave both food and fucking, she had packed the hamper and come out to the lake but even so she had not expected to really do it. She closed the hamper with a decisive snap and headed for home, feeling the tenderness of her shoulders, she sighed, knowing she would see them covered with sunburn if she looked down, not that she wanted to.

"I'm never reading a single page of that book ever again," she told herself firmly as she walked home.

Jenna lay in her bed, idly watching television and with her mind miles away from the cops and robbers series playing out before her. The book lay on the pillow beside her and she could feel herself reaching for it, wanting to touch it but she didn't.

Her eyes could not seem to stop focusing on it however. Finally, she gave in and reached for it, her fingers sliding across the pages until she came to a story whose title grabbed her attention.

Open House

The house sat back from the street on a quiet lot shaded with old trees. The sunlight washed the place with a lemony glow and as she stepped out of the passenger side of the realtor's sedate little compact. Annie Vale knew she had come home, and that to say so would ensure she did not get the good deal she was hoping for.

Margo Lewis smiled as she saw the way her client's eyes were busy taking in every detail of the place. The clients all tried to pretend they didn't like the houses they wanted. It was the easiest way to tell that they did. Unless they were just one of the complaining assholes that were simply never satisfied that often came along with the territory in the real estate business. Just the day before a woman had told her that every house she had shown her was totally unacceptable and that she would be shopping for a new realtor and home.

"I am sorry I was not able to handle your needs," Margo had said politely and in her head, she silently blessed whatever deity had seen to take mercy on her and remove the awful woman from her presence.

Looking at Annie's face as she surveyed the property she knew she was not going to be making that little speech. Looking at the swell of flesh over the lace trimmed bodice of the top Annie wore Margo found herself wanting to do a very satisfactory job of a different sort. That feeling was amplified when Annie walked slowly up the red-bricked walkway, giving Margo an opportunity to check out the plump rise of her ass, the sexy and dangerous curve of her hips and the sway of them.

Annie was not unaware that the sexy brunette realtor was checking her out. She was also aware that she was turned on by the woman. The first thing she had noticed was that while the blue skirt and jacket were severely cut and plain the jacket was worn over a sexy crisp white blouse and the pencil thinness of the skirt only served to emphasize Margo's lean flat thighs and hips. She found herself strutting a little as she stepped over the threshold of the house and was rewarded by a tiny gust of breath on the back of her neck.

"So here we have the living room area," Margo said inanely. It was the typical beginning to her spiel but she found herself unable to think of anything else to say.

Annie wandered through the airy and empty rooms, feeling her desire rise. There was not just the desire to own the house but a different sort of desire as well. Her pussy felt incredibly full and heavy and there was a slick wetness in her panties.

The kitchen had cheerful blue tiles and white paint, a long set of windows that looked out into the well-tended garden and the privacy fence, a long set of countertops and a center island.

"You could cook in this kitchen."

Annie turned to find Margo almost directly behind her. They stood there, face to face, for long awkward seconds. Margo could feel the heat of Annie's flesh; Annie could smell the subtle perfume rising from Margo's skin.

The kiss was furious. Their mouths opened as soon as their lips met. Their tongues thrust and parried, both women moaned a little as that kiss grew hotter with each second. Annie tasted peppermint; Margo could taste the chocolate Annie had eaten earlier. Both wanted more.

Annie whimpered as her clothes fell to the floor and her own hands worked to free Margo from her skirt. They paused for a moment to look at each other, and then Annie's back was pressed into the cool tile of the kitchen floor.

"Yes please." Annie whispered as teeth tugged at her nipples playfully. Margo's mouth surrounded the pink tips while her hands kneaded and squeezed the white flesh. Annie arched her back and rubbed her cunt against Margo's stocking clad knee in a desperate bid to get some relief.

Margo groaned as her fingers found the feathery soft hair at the junction of Annie's thighs. A knowing caress opened the lips beneath and a heated slickness covered Margo's questing fingers.

Annie gave in, she surrendered completely as Margo's teeth and tongue moved lower, teasing fire across her belly and upper thighs. Margo opened the juicy pink pocket of flesh, spreading the labia and licking at the salty sweet fluid there. Her tongue moved higher, she added pressure and heard Annie moan as she worked her tongue under the delicate skin of the hood and licked away creamy white beads of cum. She waited for a long moment, drawing out the pleasure of it for Annie before she took the throbbing bud of Annie's clit between her lips and began to suckle and lick at it.

Annie dug her fingers into Margo's scalp as the orgasm bloomed and spread. Her hips bucked up and down, her legs spread wider. Margo added another finger, then another, thrusting with a deliberate rhythm. The friction and the lavish attention bestowed upon her clit were so intense that she screamed, a short sharp scream, and then she came. Gooey spurts of thick white cum squirted from her pussy, ran down her ass crack and puddled on the floor beneath her while spasms wracked her body and she moaned over and over.

Margo crawled upward and found a willing mouth awaiting her. Her knees lay on the floor and she bent forward at the waist, resting on her arms as she rocked over Annie's face.

Annie licked the tender flesh gently, parting it and then sliding her tongue into the creases while her fingers found the opening and pushed their way in. She could feel the hot walls tightening around her fingers as she fucked Margo with them. Her tongue bathed Margo's clit with the same care Margo had given hers.

"Come on, fuck my face and cum on it." Annie demanded and was rewarded with a gush of sticky sweet fluid, which she drank eagerly.

When the orgasm finally ended Margo half fell to one side and a wild whoop of laughter burst from Annie.

"It's an eat-in kitchen!" She cried and Margo, caught by surprise, burst into giggles as well. "Would you like to see the bedroom?" Margo asked as she stood.

Annie looked at the long lines of Margo's body and her mouth twitched with an impish grin.

"Would I? Hell yes I would."

"Well, come with me then."

Annie followed her.

Jenna gasped and reached over to her nightstand. She pulled out the vibrator and a bottle of lube. She slicked the huge circular tip of the toy and then she rubbed more of the lube across her pussy lips, feeling the stuff mixing with her own juices. The whirr of the vibrator made her wriggle, her hips arching up higher as she strained forward, her eyes going wide as the friction on her clit became almost too much to bear.

Her free hand began to move, thrusting her fingers in and out of her hot hole. She drew her knees up higher, gasping and pleading to the ceiling as an orgasm began to flood through her.

Cum spilled from her in creamy rivulets, dripping down her ass crack and onto the sheets below her. Sweat popped up on her forehead and she thrashed wildly for a few moments, digging her heels into the mattress and crying out in a high keening voice until she finally dropped back against the mattress, her eyes closing in an undeniable languor.

"I am never reading so much as a page from that book ever again," Jenna muttered and then she fell asleep.

Jenna was sitting at the desk in her living room the next morning and the book was lying face down on the side of her desk where she kept her tissues and a picture of her ex-lover. She kept the picture as a reminder not to fall in love with someone on the first date ever again, not out of a sense of sentimentality.

She knew that she had a lot of work to do but she could not seem to get interested in it. She kept fiddling about with the keys on her laptop and groaning every time she made a mistake, which was often.

Finally, in a huff, she snatched the book up and began to read...

The Sound Of Rain

The early morning rain slashed down onto the avenue and a group of tourists chattered in excited tones as they stood in a careless clump in the middle of a sidewalk, not realizing that that alone marked them as outsiders. New Yorkers never stood still in the center of anything, much less a sidewalk.

Max stood under the meager shelter of a doorway, her hazel eyes assessing the delicately rusted curves of a black wrought iron head and foot board that someone had tossed out onto the curb. The rain glistened off one dangerous looking point of a flower that had been cast into the design and a long smile creased her face as she considered the possibilities unfolding before her.

One of the tourists laughed as she wrestled the headboard into the doorway of her apartment building, before dashing back out for the footboard. She gave them a merry finger and wondered if she told them that to city dwellers rescuing things from the curb came as naturally as paying outrageous prices for theatre tickets if they would believe it.

The headboard proved to be more difficult to maneuver than she had thought it would be. She was afraid someone else would snag her prize so she left it leaning against one wall inside the apartment's main foyer while she retrieved the footboard. The laughing tourist was walking away with his group and for one moment, Max wondered where they were from, how they had decided to bite the Big Apple for their vacation, and in the middle of February no less when the weather was at its most inclement.

She put those thoughts aside as she wrestled the bulky frame first to the elevator, then inside it and down the narrow hallway to the apartment she shared with Catherine, her partner and lover of ten years. She got the two pieces inside and then ran back outside for the rails, hoping they were still there and to her relief they were.

The apartment was half living space,

half studio. Catherine's huge battered old writing desk sat under one of the oversized windows, Max's painting space took up the space beyond the second of the windows in the old fired brick wall.

Their bed was a mattress and box springs that sat on the floor, they had been planning to buy a bed forever but other things kept that from happening. Max had had a few shows at galleries downtown and Catherine had numerous sales in anthologies and magazines but neither could afford to quit their day jobs. When Max had lost hers the month before it had taken all of the money they had been saving up to pay the missing half of the rent. She had gotten another job but so far, the fund had not been replenished.

The rails were sturdy, the head and footboard whole. The bed could be a thing of beauty if cared for properly. She mixed paint while she considered every inch of heavy iron, every airy curve of flower and fanciful curlicue that adorned the headboard. Her eyes, always searching for beauty and light and shape, took stock while her hands worked of their own accord.

The day slid away as she worked with sandpaper and quick drying paint. The light stayed the same watery grey but went more slate and charcoal colored at the edges as the winter twilight crept down from the rooftops and into the city streets.

The locks rattled and the door opened to reveal a slight figure in a sopping wet pink raincoat. Max loved to tell everyone the story of how she found Catherine in a strange little boutique hawking handbags that had been hand painted by a woman who called herself the Great Caro and wore a huge purple turban. The Great Caro had hired Max to paint dresses to match the bags and she had. One day the Great Caro had fired Catherine and she had run after her, she had chased the storming little redhead for nine blocks just to ask if she could walk her home.

On the wall between their two workspaces hung a picture of Catherine as seen from behind; a pale violet dress whipping around thin legs and brightly colored rain boots, hair whipping like a flag and determination in every line. It was the image Max had seen as she had chased her down that windy and cold afternoon.

She stood there looking at the flush of pink across Catherine's cheeks, the water puddled on the hardwood floor beneath her feet and the sea green eyes that were staring at the bed with a kind of rapt wonder.

"I used the fabric you bought to make the sheets; we didn't have any that fit."

Catherine's right eyebrow twitched

upwards, "I love it when you make it fit."

"I know you do," Max said in the most noncommittal tone she could manage but Catherine was not fooled by it.

"I want to try it out." Catherine announced.

Max watched as she stripped a piece of clothing away with every few steps. Pale tits capped by nipples that were stiff from cold and desire were bared, then a thin waist and belly. Gingery hair covered pink folds of skin with coarse curls. Flat thighs and lean hips, pretty feet, all were revealed as she made her way to her lover and the enormous bed that was a masterpiece of carefully sanded and painted black iron and crimson covers.

Their mouths met. Max tangled her fingers into Catherine's hair and lifted her face up to hers so she could plunder the wet mouth more easily. Catherine responded by arching her back and grinding her pelvis against Max's crotch.

Catherine moaned when Max slid her hands down the long column of her spine and then cupped the cool flesh of her ass, raising her up higher, onto her tiptoes. She could feel her skin warming as Max forced her thigh between her legs.

"Please," she breathed as she rubbed herself across the blue jean clad expanse of well-muscled thigh. Pussy juice leaked out and turned the denim a darker blue.

Max whispered, "You like that sweetie?"

Not waiting for a reply she bent her heads and took one of Catherine's hardened nipples into her mouth. It grew tighter even as it warmed. She sucked harder, relishing the taste of rain and skin.

They hung there suspended for a long moment then Max grabbed Catherine's arms and spun her own body sideways, using a self-defense moved they had learned years ago to pick her lover up off the floor and send her sailing onto the bed. It was a move that never failed to excite them.

The bed squeaked and moaned, Catherine squealed as well, delighted with the sudden height and the fact that bed was warmer off the floor. She opened her mouth to say so but forgot to because Max chose that moment to shed her own clothes and follow her into bed.

Max took a leisurely path down the tender and tasty body laid out before her. She kneaded the small tits and bit at the skin behind the shell pink ear. Her teeth tugged at flesh and her hands slid down curves. Each caress made Catherine shiver, which was exactly what she had had in mind.

She bent her head to the nest of red curls and used her tongue to split the seam of plump pink pussy. Her tongue delved into the slippery slit and then ran leisurely back up along it to the hood. Pearly white drops of come rolled from under the hood when she lazily flicked her tongue against it. Her teeth were gentle as she bit and sucked at the throbbing nub of clit, then her tongue rubbed against it in a demanding movement.

She licked sugary salt from the folds of the labia. She held them open with her fingers, marveling as she always did at the delicate wing-like beauty of them.

"Please," Catherine whimpered as her body arched helplessly upwards, "Please Max, please let me come, that feels so good."

"Fuck my face sweetie." Max ordered. "Come on, give it to me."

Catherine's body strained, her hips bucked against Max's greedy mouth, her fingers slid down the hard planes of her face and she moaned as she felt the strong muscles of her jaw moving beneath her fingertips.

"Will you fuck me while I come?"

Max let her fingers answer for her. She slid first one, then two deep inside the tight walls of her lover and began to move them in a fierce and steady rhythm, creating a delicious and unbearable friction.

Come spilled from Catherine's pussy, streaking her thighs with a glistening and sticky whiteness. Max kept her hands and tongue working, enjoying the feel of heated pussy shuddering around her.

She was not done yet though. She came up from her position of worship and reached for the drawer of the nightstand. Her harness made a merry jangle as she buckled it on and she took her time doing so, enjoying the way that Catherine's eyes followed every movement as she placed the large cock just so and stood there.

Both of them liked the dichotomy of the cock on her woman's body, the dizzying juxtaposition of womanly curves and muscular angles interrupted by a hard cock jutting up from the thick mat of black hair that lay at the junction of her thighs.

Catherine sat up and scooted to the edge of the bed, then slid to the floor. That kneeling pose always turned Max on and she felt an urgent desire long before Catherine opened her full lips and took the cock in.

Max rocked her hips slowly at first, then faster, her heart began to pick up speed and her breath grew harsh as she watched Catherine suck her cock. The sight of the thick hardness being swallowed so lovingly coupled with the pressure the base of the cock put on her clit made her come in a thick gush. Her come spilled onto the leather of the harness and she moaned, her fingers digging into tender scalp as she held her willing captive close.

The bed took their weight again and Max raised herself on her strong forearms, her eyes closing in concentration as she thrust into the wet heat, driving herself in deeper while Catherine wrapped her legs around her waist, urging her on. The bed creaked and sighed beneath them, the rain tapped onto the window and mingled with the sound of flesh meeting flesh as they fucked harder and harder, straining and grunting against each other's body.

The scent of sex drifted up, teasing their noses. Max kissed the hollows of Catherine's temple, then her soft mouth, forcing the lips apart with her own tongue so that her lover could taste the remains of her own come.

Max liked to watch the cock sliding in and out of the opening, liked to see the wetness glinting off it and she raised herself higher and bent her head so that she could see that. Her pussy throbbed pleasantly as the cock rubbed once more at her clit and she bit at her bottom lip, trying to concentrate on making sure her lover finished first.

"I want to come," Catherine panted out.

"Then come right now." Max rasped out as she plunged deeper and harder, "Come right now when I do baby. Come for me."

They both arched and strained. The

sound of flesh meeting flesh grew louder with every thrust. Max watched the crimson tide flow up Catherine's cheeks, and smiled when she let out a sobbing whimper, riding her harder as the body below hers shook and arced, hips slamming forward in desperation as the friction broke.

"I'm coming! Oh Max, Max, please I want ...I need you so much."

Max bit her bottom lip as her own orgasm broke over her. Her ass cheeks clenched and her breath hitched in and out in a thick wheeze as she went rigid, then curled into a question mark shape.

They lay there, Max's cock still inside Catherine's pussy. Juices dripped from both of them, making a sticky mess of their tangled limbs and the covers beneath them.

"We need food." Max finally said as she pulled out and then she nibbled on Catherine's ear.

Giggles rose from the bed, "I would have thought you had had enough to eat sweetie."

"I'm a growing boy." Max stroked the soaked belly of the cock to give meaning to the words.

"I think you are big enough."

They both laughed at that sally.

"I agree. But if we don't get up and go get food I am going to starve to death."

Catherine started to protest, the idea of going out on such a foul night was hardly appealing, especially with such a nice warm bed beneath her body.

"How did you get this bed anyway?"

"Curb rescue."

Catherine wondered how she had gotten it upstairs and into the apartment alone but did not ask, Max was the stronger of them, without a doubt. She was the one who killed the spiders and fearlessly dealt with obnoxious people who had nasty things to say about two women holding hands. She always wondered how a woman so tough could be so gentle but she never asked because it would have upset Max.

They had developed a balance, Catherine thought sleepily. And part of that balance was repaying the gift of a bed by going out into the windy evening despite not wanting to.

They got up and dressed. Max watched Catherine putting on her pink raincoat and bright boots and a long grin crossed her face. She wanted some fresh made pasta, a rich and garlic-laden sauce, hot crusty bread and a bottle of red wine. A crisp salad and a slightly sweet white cheese and there was a tiny place a few blocks down where they could get that very meal for a very reasonable price.

They stepped out into the night.

Holding hands under a brightly striped umbrella, they set off down the avenue, both of them thinking that later there would be the sound of rain. And bed.

Jenna gave up. She stood up and slid her clothes off, her hands running madly across her body. Her fingers found her nipples and she flicked them, closing her eyes in sheer enjoyment as she did so. They swelled under her fingers and she whimpered a bit, bumping her hips forward slightly as her head fell back and her eyes closed in utter surrender.

She slid her fingers down the curves of her belly, enjoying the feel of it lying flat and soft beneath her questing hand. The mound of her pussy rose up and she glided her palm over it, feeling the softness of her thin curls and the slippery fluids that were already leaking around the edges of the puffy pink lips that hid the deeper recesses of her cunt.

A finger slid inside that wet heat and she arched forward, straining to feel the friction, then she withdrew that finger and stuck it in her mouth, sucking at it with delighted bliss.

She put her finger back inside herself, raising a leg onto the low ottoman as she did so, it opened her up further. Cool air met her pussy and made her quiver, she began to hump and thrust faster, her legs shaking as she visualized the hot sex between the two women in the story. She began to whisper to herself as she used her free hand to smack her own ass. The hard spanks made her pussy throb with desire and she could feel her nipples hardening as her orgasm neared.

Come spooled down the inside of her thighs and dripped onto her hardwood floors; she gasped and shuddered a final time before collapsing in a chair and taking a few long and deep breaths.

Her phone rang a few minutes later and she opened her eyes and checked the number, then answered.

"Hi Carrie, how are you?"

"I am fine, are you still buried out there in the sticks?" Came the cheerful voice of her best friend. "What the hell do you do out there all day long?"

"Read," Jenna said with a nasty grin. "I do a lot of reading."

5 FORBIDDEN FRIENDS

Tommy Dundee was a bright young man. He was good-looking, he was muscular, and he had just turned 18. On that magical day when he became an adult, he got up from his bed, walked to the bathroom of his father's small ramshackle house in his briefs, brushed his teeth, washed his face, and then went to his room to get dressed. He had already packed a small bag with the most basic things that mattered to him, and he picked it up. He walked through the house that had been the only home that he had ever known one last time. He walked past his father's bedroom door and peeked inside.

The man who had given him life was

also the man who had made it so miserable. Now that man was lying on his bed, flat on his back, buck-naked, his cock as hard as a rock. He was passed out solid, sleeping off the drunk from the night before. That was nothing new. He got drunk about every night and had for as long as Tommy could remember. Tommy looked at his father's large beefy body, his hairy hulking form lying there exposed and vulnerable. His manhood was swollen and was pointing strongly at the ceiling; the foreskin of his cock pulled slightly back, revealing the end of his massive knob underneath.

His father's balls, large and hairy, hung low in his sack between his splayed-out legs. Those balls were where he came from 18 years prior. His dad breathed slowly but loudly as he lay spread-eagled on the bed. Tommy pulled the door closed. That was how he wanted to remember the man whom he would never see again: a massive piece of impressive manhood, lying dormant. Not the raucous asshole that was bitter and chided everyone he encountered when he was sober and that was violent and abrasive when he was drunk. Tommy walked out of the house and never looked back.

The next day Tommy was walking down the highway, hitching a ride and trying his best just to make it out of the state of

Oklahoma as fast as possible. He had already made it five counties away from the bastard father whom he had left behind. He was thumbing his way when a red Ford pickup pulled alongside him. He ran to the passenger door and got inside. The man driving it was a rancher named Jack Miller. Jack had asked him what the Sam Hill he was doing hitching a ride in the middle of March at his age.

"I am heading out to California to be with some family out there and maybe get into a good school," Tommy said.

"I see. And you think that you're gonna just walk your ass all the way to California. Didn't it occur to you to get on a bus or a train, boy?" Jack asked.

"It did, sir, but I ain't got any money. My old man was...well he ain't around for me now anymore and I ain't got anything here to stay for. I figure I can head out there and get a new life going. They say that California is a good place for that, where everything can start new," Tommy said.

"Yeah, I suppose that's true if that's what you're looking for, but then I ain't got any need or want to start anything new at my age. I'm just happy with how I am. So how long do you think you'll have to walk to get there?" Jack asked laughingly.

"I don't know, but I know I'll do what I have to do to get away from here. I just turned 18 yesterday, and I don't want the next 18 years to be stuck here like the first ones were."

Jack looked at him and wondered what could be driving a young man like him to take such drastic measures. It seemed impetuous, it seemed extreme, and Jack was sure that there would be someone who would go looking for him soon enough—someone who cared enough to look. He figured he had to do something as a good God-fearing man, if nothing else to help the kid out.

"I tell you what boy: if you want to, I have a ranch about five miles up the way here. I will make you a deal. It ain't wise to be taking off like this on a whim, and it certainly ain't good to do it flat fuckin' ass broke. I need some help around my place. I will give you a job and a place to sleep, wash up, and eat. I'll even pay you some cash, say $75 a week. If you'll work for me through the end of August, I'll get you that bus or train ticket to California, and when you get going out there, you'll have a pocket of cash to help you get going on your way. Sounds to me like it would work out good for both of us," Jack said as he looked over at the kid. If nothing else, it might buy him some time to help figure out whom the kid was running from and why and maybe straighten the whole thing out.

Tommy thought about it. He could use the money, and five counties was a good distance away, maybe enough that his asshole dad wouldn't find him if he started looking. He looked at the big, burly rancher. He didn't know why, but he liked the way that he looked. He found that he liked the way that some guys looked, but he never really liked looking at pretty girls. He didn't know what that was; he thought that maybe he was queer, but this wasn't the place to try to find out. That could get a fella killed.

"Sure! I guess that's OK. I mean if you need the help all that bad, I could use the money. OK," Tommy said, and Jack smiled.

They headed to the big rancher's place. That evening Tommy was standing by the bathtub looking in the mirror; he was in his undershorts, a pair of tighty-whities. Jack came upstairs and saw him standing there looking at himself in the mirror. He started to turn his eyes down so as not to invade the young man's privacy since he was in his underwear, but as he did, Tommy turned his back to him to turn off the water that was filling the tub.

Despite the young man being in his briefs, Jack could not look away. His eyes were locked on the back of Tommy. Specifically, he was looking at the large red whelps and deep purple-black bruises that were all over the young man's back and the rear of his legs. As Tommy slid his tighty-whities down his legs and removed them from around his feet, Jack saw that there were old scars on his ass cheeks, the kind that comes from having your skin laid open with a piece of cane. There were dozens of them.

Jack slowly made his way backwards down the stairs until he was sure that he was out of view but could still see into the bathroom. Tommy turned and Jack got a good look at his front. More bruises, more whelps, more scars. There were even scars on his long, thick hanging manhood. He didn't have a foreskin like a normal fella should; instead he had a jagged, harsh scar around the shaft of his pecker. The only thing Jack could figure out is that whoever had hurt him had taken his man cover with a pocketknife.

The thought made Jack sick. Who would do such a thing, such a retched thing to a young buck at the start of his life? Someone had beaten this boy bad, and often, for a very long time. He was furious. He understood now why someone would want to run from that kind of life. And he was determined to help the guy in any way that he could. He remembered that the kid said his "old man was...well he ain't around for me now anymore." He figured it was dear old daddy who had done those things and left those marks on his own son. He even damaged his own son's manhood. It was disgusting. Jack was furious. Tommy closed the bathroom door, and he heard him get into the tub.

Over the next several months, it turned out that Tommy was hell of a worker. He was up at sunrise, worked all day, and washed up, being careful not to let Jack see him naked. Then after dinner, he and Jack would sit on the porch, drinking beer and talking. Over time Jack got Tommy to open up and gradually Jack learned the whole truth. Things were getting smoother between the two when one day, Jack knew he had to confront Tommy about the scars. He waited until Tommy was getting washed up, and when he knew that he was naked, he then came into the bathroom with no warning. He looked all over the boy, who was standing nude before him.

"He put those scars on you, didn't he, Tommy?" he asked. Tommy just nodded his head.

"And he cut your skin off your Johnny, didn't he?" he asked. Tommy held his tool in his hand and looked down at it; he looked back up at Jack.

"Yes sir. When I turned 16, he did it

'cause he was drunk and he saw me pulling on it too much after I took a piss," he said.

"Damn it boy. That ain't how a man should treat his son. You're safe here now. You don't have to run to California if you don't want to. You're welcome to stay here as long as you want. I can keep you on year-round if you'd like. You're a good worker, and...well, you need someone to be good to you," Jack said.

He embraced the young man right then and held him while Tommy cried onto his shirt-covered shoulder. For the next hour, Tommy cried and cried, and Jack held him close. His heart was broken for the boy; he had never been able to make children with his late wife. But if he had, he would have wanted the boys to turn into men like Tommy was.

Over the next few months, things got even closer between the two. There were some things that Tommy would occasionally do that caught Jack off guard—times when he would see him watching him, looking at him wash up naked or take a piss behind the barn. It wasn't anything serious, but over time he had to start questioning it, especially after one incident when he was stripped naked, as he was on the day he was born, washing mud and grime off of himself after fighting with a pig in the pen. He could swear he saw Tommy watching him and rubbing on his own crotch. He tried to pass it off, figuring that since his bone was standing up big and proud, the young man was just getting his up to maybe make a comparison. A bad idea for the young man, as Jack was as well hung as the horses he had in the barn, but if he wanted to compare, he couldn't stop him. "His daddy probably never showed him what a grown man looked like down below," he figured.

Summer was soon drawing to a close, and one night near the end of August, Jack and Tommy were sitting on the front porch, drinking beer and talking as usual. Jack reached into his pocket and took out a bus ticket for San Francisco, California. He handed it to Tommy. "I told you that at the end of summer, I could pay you up whatever I owed you and then I'd also get you that ticket. It's yours. But I also told you a couple of months ago that if you wanted to stay here for good, I would keep you on. The choice is yours, Tommy."

Tommy looked at the ticket and smiled. He wasn't sure what he wanted to do. He saw that the ticket was undated so it was not as if he had to decide immediately. He sat it on the table beside the porch swing he was sitting on. Jack was on a rocker with his big booted feet up on the rail of the porch. He was wearing a clean pair of jeans, a clean shirt that was open all the way down to reveal his muscular, hairy chest, and his white felt cowboy hat. He had his can of beer nestled against the fly of his well-packed jeans. The scent of his masculinity was obvious to Tommy despite the fact that the young man was several feet away. Tommy liked the way that Jack smelled. He was always able to pick the big man's scent up when he was anywhere near him.

It was almost an hour after dinner that they spent talking before the conversation came to a pause. Jack knew that there was a chance that Tommy would take the ticket and leave, but he wasn't sure. If he did, there was something that he needed to get straight with the young man before he left, and he figured this was as good a time as any to address it. It could be his last chance.

"Tommy, I need to ask you something, and I don't want it to be a major thing between us, but I really would like an honest answer," Jack said as he sat with his boots up on the railing of the porch.

"Sure Jack, what is it? After everything that you have done for me, I would never consider lying to you or holding anything back about anything," Tommy said.

"Look, a few weeks ago, I was washing up behind the barn, and I noticed you standing over behind the bushes, hiding and watching me. I guess I had seen you doing stuff like that before but didn't really pay much attention to it, but that time, I saw you rubbing yourself, down on the front of your britches. Since then, I have been keeping an eye on how you act around me, and I have to admit that I see you watching me do stuff, man stuff, more than what I can casually brush off. Tommy, are you queer?" Jack asked. The look on the younger man's face was one of shock and shame. He had tried so hard to be not obvious when he was watching Jack. He had not been careful enough it seemed.

"To be honest with you, sir, I don't know. I guess I might be. I had never done anything like that, and really before you, I haven't even taken the trouble to do any watching of fellas. I might be, but I don't know. If you're pissed, I am sorry, Jack. It's just that you're... well you're more of a man than anyone I think I have ever known, and I don't have anybody to go to with things about sex and what I'm feeling. I thought that if I watched you, I might be able to find some answers to all this stuff in my heart that got me all twisted up, but the more I did it, the more I found myself getting bothered up by you," Tommy said as he looked out into the dark Oklahoma night.

He thought so highly of Jack that he was suddenly heartbroken that his secret was out. He knew that this would be the end of the friendship that they had started to enjoy. Jack looked out at the night sky as well; the stars were bright, as was the moon, but there were heavy clouds moving in. The air smelled like rain. Sure enough, about 10 minutes later, not a word being spoken between the men in the meantime, the sky was filled with clouds and a light drizzle was falling. The rail of the porch was getting wet with the drops of rain that were coming down, and Jack moved his feet off of it and planted them on the porch deck, spread wide. He held his beer can in his hands and looked at the label. He put the can to his lips and turned it up, downing the rest of the strong bitter brew in one gulp. He looked over at Tommy, who was sitting there with a crushed look on his face. The kid looked like he had just confessed to murder and was awaiting his death sentence to be passed down.

"Tommy, I don't understand what it is that you feel when you look at a fella like me, especially when I'm doing stuff that is supposed to be private and the like. But I guess it's the same thing that I feel when I looked at a pretty girl when I was at your age. You say that you have never done anything that was queer and that no other fella ever got your switch flipped like I do. I guess I rightly should take that as a compliment and be flattered. The thing is that I don't know how to respond to that sort of thing. I haven't ever had any inkling in that direction. I do know this, though. I took you in here to help make a man out of you and turn a kid into an adult that was able to go off and live a life that was worth something. You have more than matured in my book to be sure, but you're right. There ain't anyone else around to help you out with that kind of thing. This ain't California, and it ain't New York City. But I suppose I would call myself a failure if I didn't finish the job that I started out to do, and this is a right big part of it. The truth be told, I kind of feel really connected to you too. I don't know why and I'm damn sure that it ain't the same type of feelings that you feel for me.... Then again, maybe it is, and I don't know how to go about feeling 'em but I will tell you this. If you want what it is that you have been thinking about and we both understand that this is a one-time run, then I'll let you have it and I'll give it to you as good as my broken-down rancher's body and ol' pussy pounder can lay out for ya. So what do you say, boy? Do you want what it is that you have been feeling to happen tonight or not? I don't know why in tarnation I'm saying this, but I'm up to it if you are," Jack said.

The look on Tommy's face was blank. He could not believe what the big masculine rancher was saying: if he wanted to have sex with him, then he would go along and do it. He was speechless.

"Mr. Miller...Jack, I...I don't know what to say. I mean are you sure?"

"Boy, I wouldn't have made the offer if I wasn't sure. I don't know how the hell this kind of thing works, but I'm here and so are you. I suppose that it can't be too far different from how it works with a woman. I mean it's just to slide my rod into the hole, pull out, and repeat, ain't it? Pretty simple to me," Jack said.

Tommy nodded his head in agreement with the statement. He didn't have to say another word. Jack could see the front of the younger man's pants by the way that he was sitting, and he was as stiff as a tire iron underneath them. He had his answer, and he figured there was no better time or way to deal with this than to just jump in with both feet right now. He stood up and walked over to where Tommy was sitting on the swing and sat down beside him. The young man looked at him deeply in his eyes with a confused and scared look.

"Boy, you've seen me naked and I've seen you too. There ain't any secrets in that way, but you know that I am a biggie. I've been with five women in my life, and all of them got hurt when I was done with 'em on the first go. The question here is, are you sure you are good for this?" Jack asked.

Tommy just nodded.

"Good. Then I don't see no reason to wait any longer," Jack said as he leaned over. And after tilting his cowboy hat back, he placed one hand on Tommy's cheek and the other on the back of his head and connected their mouths together in a deep passionate kiss. Jack's tongue danced slowly and tenderly inside of Tommy's mouth. It was the first kiss that he had given to anyone after six years since his wife passed on. It felt good to be doing it despite the foreign nature of the feelings he had for the person that he was kissing.

As the two men kissed, Tommy let his hands move up to rest against the hairy chest of the big rancher stud. He started to rub the rancher's chest under his flannel shirt, letting the wiry, thick hair move between his fingers. He opened his eyes and saw that Jack had his eyes open as well. The kiss broke, and Tommy started to blush.

"There ain't anything shameful here, boy. We both feel that this is something that needs to happen so we just need to let that happen. Your touch is nice. It's the first time that I have had someone to touch me since Janet died. I want...no, I need you to touch me all over. Especially down there," Jack said as he took Tommy's hand in his own and slowly slid it down his front to the swollen mass of manhood that was lumped up behind the fly of his tight jeans.

He was not hard, but he was on his way. Tommy could feel the heat from the big man's groin through the heavy-denim jeans. He leaned forward, and the two men kissed again. Tommy felt himself getting even harder in his own pants. His hand moved to Jack's back and started to rub his muscular, wide shoulder through the soft cotton shirt.

"Jack, I don't know what to do. I have no idea how this is supposed to happen," Tommy said.

"Neither do I, boy, but we will figure it out. I ain't ever been with a fella, but I've been with women, and if you'll let me be in charge here, I think I might be able to teach you a few things about how to get down to the nasty of human mating."

Tommy made the first move; he slid down off of the swing and onto his knees between the legs of the rancher stud. He had heard people at school talk about certain sexual things, and he knew that one of the things that he wanted to do with Jack was to take him into his mouth and pleasure him in an amazing way. He rubbed his hands all over the denim-covered legs and heavy cowboy boots of the big older man before he moved his fingers to the waistband of Jack's pants.

Tommy opened the belt of Jack as he settled in between the rancher's legs. Jack had heard about what he was sure the young man was about to do. He had even had a young woman offer to do it for him in the back of Jasper's bar in town one night, but he had declined as he was not one for making his whoopee in a public place and it was far too late to head to her house for the evening.

Now Tommy had his jeans open, and the front of his white broadcloth boxer shorts was tented out with the massive 10 inches of his manhood. Tommy popped the two snaps on the fly and the boxers sprung open, letting Jack's man-snake out into the warm night air. Tommy moved his hand up and slid back the rancher's long droopy foreskin. Jack was heartbroken that the retraction of his tool cover, something that almost every man considers an extremely pleasurable thing to happen, was a feeling that Tommy would never feel on his fully matured adult organ. For that reason alone, he wished that he could track down Tommy's father and do the same thing to him that he had done to his son.

Tommy leaned forward and stuck out his tongue. He started to lick the large shiny purple head of Jack's organ, licking the heavy drip of precum off of the end and then flicking his tongue across the tightly stretched banjo string on the underside of the head. Jack tensed up and let out a moan of pleasure as Tommy flicked his tongue tip back and forth over the supersensitive sweet spot of his cock.

Tommy worked his mouth up and down the length of the big rancher's massive man pole. He took him deep into his throat several times, and it was a feeling that Jack never in his life thought he would feel. Being buried 10 inches deep into another man's throat was like having his thick pussy probe slid into the tightest virgin twat that he could ever imagine being able to mount up on. Jack found himself holding the back of Tommy's head and grinding his hips forward to force himself all the way inside the other man's mouth.

He was breathing hard, and he felt like his heart was about to explode out of his chest. Soon he felt himself getting to the point that he was gonna let go of his seed, and he didn't want this to end that soon or in that way. He wanted to take the virginity of the young man who had lusted for him for so long. He wanted to man up and mount up on the 18-year-old's back hole, and he needed to do that soon. He pulled himself out of Tommy's mouth and looked down at the young ranch hand.

"My God, boy! That was the most incredible thing that I have ever felt. I didn't even know that a fella could feel that good by putting it in other's mouth. I ain't ever done that, but I know that I want to do it again. But now I want to show you the proper way of screwing. We can't get to that out here though. Come on to my bedroom," Jack said as he grabbed Tommy by the hand.

He led the younger man into the house and upstairs. As they moved through the house, Jack pulled his cowboy boots off and then his flannel shirt. His jeans came off next at the head of the stairs as Tommy also went about pulling clothes off of his body. By the time the two men got to the bedroom, they were both down to skivvies and socks. Jack still had his cowboy hat on his head. They had kissed as they made their way through the house, and now they kissed deeply one more time. Tommy could feel the rock-hard 10 inches of Jack pressing against his belly through the fabric of his boxers.

His own tighty-whities were stretched to the max with his heavy 7-inch prong. There was a large wet spot forming on the soft cotton of his briefs as he anticipated what was coming, although deep down, he didn't know what that was. As they broke the kiss, Jack picked Tommy up in the air and moved him to the bed before dropping him onto the mattress. The quilted bedcover that Janet had sewn for their marital bed more than three decades earlier was still on it. Jack didn't care. He finally was ready to accept that his wife was dead and he needed to move on.

He was going to fuck tonight for the first time in six years; he was going to be a real man and spread his seed. And if that defiles the quilt that she sewed for their nuptial, too damn bad. He needed to do what he needed to do; he had mourned long enough, and he was tired of pumping his right hand up and down by himself to a vague memory. As Tommy lay on the bed, Jack looked down at him and was rampant hard. He needed to take the young man. He knew how to do this; he had done it to Janet many times when her monthly visitor prevented them from being together in the normal way.

He took his cowboy hat off, and just like what he used to do when he was with his wife, he hung it on the bedpost. He unfastened the two snaps that held the front of his boxer shorts closed, and they hit the floor around his feet. He stepped out of the underwear and stepped up to the side of the bed. Tommy lay there in his tighty-whities and looked up at the big dominative male who was about to take his virginity from him. Tommy slid his briefs down his legs and dropped them to the other side of the bed. Jack nodded. The young man's scared and skinned cock was now standing up at full size.

Jack climbed onto the bed and leaned down. He did the same thing Tommy had done to him on the front porch. He took the young stud's 18-year-old meat stick into his mouth and started to suck on it. He moved his head up and down the length of the boy's prick. He didn't know what came over him to do such a thing; not only was he naked and in bed with another man, but also he had that guy's manhood in his mouth like a cheap whore.

He was shocked at how much it tasted like when he would lick his wife's opening before mounting up on her to try to breed a child into her. They had never been successful at the act, but oh how they had fun trying. Jack was sure that the problem had been on her side as his cum was thick and white and sticky; it was so rich with sperm that it sometimes came out with clumps in it from being so potent. His wife, on the other hand, wasn't right. She would not just have one time of the month but most months two, in some cases three. Over time, she learned to take him in the back rather than leave him feeling like less than a man by not being able to undertake his husbandly rights. On those times that he was able to take her front opening, she had always been dry and closed tight. He had learned to lick her to get her wet for both of their comfort, and now that he was working the young ranch hand's meat stalk in and out of his mouth, he didn't see where this was any different really than what he had done to pleasure her.

After several minutes of sucking on Tommy's cock, Jack pulled off of him and moved back off of the bed. Tommy thought that something was wrong at first when Jack went to the bathroom. It was when he came back though that he saw why he had gone.

"I use this jelly to make getting after myself with my hand easier. I used to use it on my wife in the backside as well to not hurt her so bad from me being this big. I reckon I have to use it with you for the same reason as a butthole is a butthole, man or woman," Jack said as he popped the top off of the jar and started to smear the thick white petroleum jelly all over his long, thick man stick.

Tommy nodded and turned over onto his stomach. He spread his legs wide to let Jack have access to his ass. Jack got back up onto the bed and stopped; he grabbed his cowboy hat and put it back onto his head. He moved his fingers to the base of his giant cock and placed the end of it against the opening of Tommy's guts. "I'm sorry boy for this, but we both know that it's what you need and I guess it's what I need too. When I did this to my wife, she used to scream and holler for a few minutes, but then she would calm down and start to enjoy the hell out of it. I hope that it would be the same with you. Here it comes, Tommy!" he said as he pushed forward and his heavy cock penetrated the young man's anal ring.

Tommy let out a scream as his guts were invaded by the monster cock of Jack. The big rancher's white sock-covered feet pressed against the footboard of the bed and the whole of his almost foot-long man stick slid deep into the rectum of Tommy. "God damn! That's tight, boy. Your shitter is like a pussy from heaven," Jack said.

Tommy would normally have taken the words as a compliment, but the burning sensation and the feeling of like being torn apart was filling his mind at the moment so greatly that he didn't have time to think about compliments. Once Jack had bottomed out inside of Tommy, he stopped moving, his sock-covered feet holding him on position. His arms supported him almost like he was doing pushups, and his hips rested against Tommy's buttocks. His full 10-inch-long, beer-bottle-thick man organ was shoved to the hilt inside the 18-

year-old ranch hand's guts.

He could feel the rectal walls of Tommy massaging his pole, milking him in both directions, trying to pull him in deeper to satisfy the boy's lust and push him out of Tommy's ass to end the torment of Tommy's deflowering. He held his position and waited. He knew that it would happen soon enough, and in a few minutes, it did. The sphincter of Tommy relaxed, and Jack felt the boy's hole go from clenching and fighting to open and welcoming. Keeping his feet in position on the footboard and his arms in position on each side of Tommy's shoulders, he started to move only his hips up and down, moving his cock in and out of Tommy's hole slowly and in small movements.

Tommy started to moan and soon so was Jack. Both men were feeling the pleasure of the act now, and Tommy wanted Jack to keep it up forever. Jack would have been happy to oblige, but no man can hold out forever; in fact, it had been so long since Jack had been inside of someone that he was going to be lucky if he could last for more than 10 minutes. He started to use a full stroke now, which caused the head of his prick to slide right over that sweet, tingling nub inside the other man's butt hole. Tommy could feel his cock twitch each time that Jack's massive cock head pressed his prostate.

The little button was sending electrical charges up and down his spine with every stroke. Soon Jack knew that he would be giving in to his needs. He felt his massive baby maker tighten up in his hairy sack, and he felt this foreskin tightening around the crown of his knob, which doubled in size. The time had come. He was going to cum; he was going to spread his seed like a real man needs to.

He pushed deep and held his organ as far inside of Tommy as he could. Of course, there was no way to get Tommy pregnant, but Jack's biological drive was to do what he had to try. His body didn't know the difference between holes. He was a man, and men tried their best to breed other things. It was instinct. He let go of rope after rope of thick sperm-filled semen as deep into Tommy's guts as he could drive it. Tommy could feel the hot liquid pouring through his insides as Jack unloaded himself.

When Jack had finished recovering from his orgasm, he slid himself out of Tommy's hole and rested back on his haunches. He looked down at the butt of the young man and saw that his load of thick creamy cum was starting to drip out of the other man's insides and onto his wife's quilt. He moved to the side of the bed and caressed Tommy's back. The young man rolled on to his side and looked up at him. His 7-

inch cock was still rock-hard and throbbing with his heartbeat. Jack looked down at it.

"Well hell, in for a penny, in for a buck," he said and grabbed the tub of petroleum jelly from the side table. He handed it to Tommy. "Give me your worst buddy; just make sure that you grease that thing and my back door up damn good!" he said as he moved to position in all fours on the bed, still wearing his socks and cowboy hat.

Tommy looked at him and was not sure that he could do this to the man that he had taken such an admiration to, but the burning in his loins and the fire in his heart drove him to get up on his knees and mount the big rancher's ass just the same as he had just done to him. He fucked Jack deep and hard, and it hurt the rancher stud like hell. It didn't take long for him to start to feel the same pleasurable pressure that Tommy had felt when he was the one on the receiving end of the hard ride. Soon his 10 inches were standing back up hard, his cock fat once more and hanging down between him and the mattress top.

As Tommy got to the point of no return, Jack tensed up and shot another thick load of sperm-filled man cream all over the quilt surface. He let out a howl as Tommy grunted deep and emptied his own load of semen into Jack's guts. Both men collapsed on the bed and started to hold one another as they kissed deeply.

"I don't want you to go…," Jack said.

"Neither do I," Tommy responded. They spent the rest of the night holding and fondling each other's naked muscular bodies, falling asleep in each other's arms.

The next morning Jake awoke to the light of a new day. He sat up in bed and looked around. Tommy was not in the bed. Jack figured at first that the young man either was in the bathroom or had wandered off to do something while he slumbered away. He swung his legs out of the bed and sat on the side for a moment, looking out at the bright and sunny morning before standing up. Naked, he moved to the window, moved the sheers aside with his fingers and looked out at his ranch.

Everything seemed so bright and fresh. Everything seemed so new. There was a quiet calm inside of him that he had not felt for a very long time. He grabbed his boxer shorts off the floor where they had been discarded the night before in the midst of his passionate sexual encounter with Tommy. He still could not believe that he had done that: he had engaged in sex with another man—a man half his age. The thing was that it felt so right at the time and even now, he was not upset by the fact. Rather, looking down at the tent that his hard cock was making in his boxer shorts, he knew that he wanted to find Tommy and do it all again.

He walked out of the bedroom and down the stairs. "Tommy!" he called out to no response. "Come on, boy. I want to talk to you, among other things!" he said again as he made his way through the house. He got to the kitchen and found lying on the counter a folded letter.

Jack,

Thank you so much for everything that you did for me this summer and especially for last night. Truth be told, I have wanted and needed that to happen for a long time. I will never forget you. You have shown me that the feelings that I have had inside of me since I was 12 years old are OK and that there is a whole world to be enjoyed. The thing is that we both know that the world that I must explore is not one that exists here in Oklahoma. I think I may love you, but that cannot be, not here in this backwater place. I am heading to San Francisco, California. I will be staying at the YMCA until I can find a place. I will then leave an address for you to find me if you want to write or visit, or more. I know that you would never leave your ranch, and

I would not expect you to. If one day, however, you desire to have a special "son" in your life, I will always be proud to call you my "daddy" as the real one is a useless piece of crap and, in 18 years, never showed me half of the love and affection you did in five months. I hope that one day our paths would cross again.

Tommy

Jack walked out onto the back porch of the house in his underwear and sat down on the steps. He looked out at the dry land, the green grass, the place that he had called home for his whole life. In all of his 51 years, he had not traveled more than 400 miles from the front door of this house. That trip had been when he was in high school, him being a member of the Young Farmers of America. He didn't know why he held on so dearly to this place. It might have been Janet. It might have been his parents, his father whom he had turned into many years ago. He was even wearing the same damn solid white boxer shorts his father wore. Truth be told, he hated boxer shorts. He would rather wear briefs like those that Tommy did—like he did when he was Tommy's age.

He held onto the life that he had here because he didn't know that there was anything else real out there but this life. Now he knew that was not true. He knew that there was a life that was out there for him, which, just like Tommy said, could not be in this place. He felt the power and heat of having a naked man's body pressing against his, and he knew that he wanted to feel that again. He knew that he wanted to feel the driving of another man's pecker in and out of his hole and that he wanted to feel the smooth, tight muscles of another man as he gave the same treatment to him. He looked down at the letter.

I think I may love you...

I am heading to San Francisco, California. I will be staying at the YMCA until I can find a place...

If one day, however, you desire to have a special "son" in your life, I will always be proud to call you my "daddy"...

I hope that one day our paths would cross again...

"I hope they do too, son. I really do. In fact...," he said as he got up and looked out at the ranch one more time. There were so many memories over the years, but right now the only ones that filled his mind were from the last five months, the ones with Tommy. He turned and walked into the house. He picked up the phone and called Graham Hudson.

"Hudson, it's Miller. Look, I may be leaving town for a while, perhaps a long while. What would you give me for my cattle and land use rights to my place for, say, the next year?... I see. Well, that is more than fair, I suppose, and more than enough for my needs to be sure. Would you be interested in making arrangements to renew the land use if I desired to hold onto this place but not be here for the long term after 12 months is up?... OK then I tell you what, get the money together and have your fancy ass lawyer you love so much draw up something. I'll meet you at the bank, say, tomorrow afternoon.... No, I really need to be getting myself out as soon as possible. No, nothing like that. Just ah... well let's just say it's a family emergency. I will be out of town for at least the next 10–12 months and maybe longer, depending on how things go.... Yeah, I'm going to San Francisco. Got some family out there that I need to be with for a while."

6 BAREBACK PORN STORE ADVENTURES

Memphis, TN, is a city that is filled with contrasts. The city is very conservative on the whole, and yet it has one of the largest gay and lesbian populations in the entire southeastern United States. I love living here as I am a gay man, and I love living in this town. It's not like the other major gay cities where the gay lifestyle is in your face 24/7 everywhere you look. Here, things are very active but very quiet. That's perfect for me since I am so far in the closet that I am finding Christmas presents from the year I was born. That is what makes my job so much fun. I am the manager of a large adult entertainment center in the heart of the city. At one time, the Athens Bookstore and Theater was the premier adult outlet in the region; these days, it's still popular but not like it used to be. There is still a very busy crowd of men that make use of the theater and the video arcade booths on a regular basis, and with me being the manager, I have unrestricted access and a damn good reason to be in those areas any time that I want to and for the most part I get to go unnoticed. This allows me to not only play as much as I like but to also watch a lot of other play that goes on in the store.

I recently had a chance to observe an interesting encounter in the video arcade. The back room of the store has two doors that allow access, one from the arcade hallway and one from the shop floor. I was sweeping out the back room with the doors open when I saw movement in the arcade corridor. As I looked up, I saw a huge muscle bear walking down the hallway very casually. He was stopping every now and then, glancing into the booths. It was not as if he was looking for anything specific, but rather, he had the appearance of "window shopping." After a few minutes, he found a booth that he was happy with, one which had the "in-use" light turned off. He entered the booth, but he did not slide the privacy curtain closed. This is a well-known signal in the store for a man who was looking to have a good tie. I have a particular soft spot in my heart for big and burley bears like him, and I was just about to step over to that booth and see if he wanted a little company, when I saw more movement in the hallway. There was another man, a young, good-looking twink, starting to walk down the hallway checking out the activity in the open booths and skipping over the ones that had closed curtains. He got to the booth that had the bear inside of it. He stopped and waited for a moment. He then stepped inside and closed the curtain behind him. I figured that this was about to get interesting, so I dropped my broom and headed for the booth directly beside the one that the big bear and the good-looking twink were in. I closed the curtain and slid down to my knees on the floor next to the wall. I put my eye up to the glory hole that had been bored in the partition between the booths a long time ago and only made bigger with time.

As I looked though the glory hole, I saw the twink rubbing his hands all over the chest and belly of the bear. The big bear was wearing a black and yellow plaid flannel shirt, and a pair of camo pants. On his feet, he was wearing a heavy pair of black leather combat boots, and he had a white ball cap on his head with the logo of the University of Memphis Fighting Tigers football team on it. Anyone who saw him enter that booth would suspect that the guy was there to watch a quick porno of some hot chick getting banged hard by some big-dicked muscle stud. They would never suspect that he was actually there to get down and dirty with another man for an afternoon quickie. He had a full beard that was neatly trimmed, and his salt and pepper hair was cropped close. He was built big and tough looking with broad shoulders and a barrel chest. He had a full beer belly but was not by any means fat. His arms were long and large. He had the cuffs of the shirt sleeves rolled up, and his very hairy forearms were covered with tribal tattoos. The twink rubbed his hands over the flannel-covered chest of the bear. The bear was whispering something to the twink as he held the smaller, younger man by his hips and swayed back and forth with him slowly, almost as if they were going to start dancing at any moment. Suddenly, the bear stopped whispering and spoke clearly.

"You like big men don't you boy?" The big bear said.

"Yes sir, I love big men, real men. I love to feel them holding me, using me, breeding me?" The twink said.

"Well hell boy, if that's what you are looking for, I can give you that and a whole lot more; why don't you show me how much you like big men right now?"

The bear said.

"Yes sir." The twink responded as he slid down the big brute's body and got to his knees on the dirty concrete floor. The bears hands rested on his shoulders and guided him down as he lowered himself to a kneel position. When he was on his knees and settled in, the bear's hands started to caress the back of the twink's head. He ran his thick, heavy fingers through the shocks of bright blond hair on the smaller man's skull. The twink reached up and started to unfasten the big man's belt. He unbuttoned the top three buttons on the bear's pants when the bear pushed his hands away.

"No not yet, boy. You said you love big men, real men. Show me how much you love us, worship me boy, and make me feel the love," he said as he held the young man chin in his hand. The twink nodded and moved further down toward the floor. He started to kiss the big bear's boots, rubbing his hands all over the leather and licking the shiny, highly polished toes. After he had worked over both boots, front and back, he started to make his way up the big bear's thick legs. His hands ran up and down the heavy camo-printed canvas fabric as he kissed the big man's legs every couple of inches. The twink made his way back up to the crotch of the bear. The big man's pants were now wide open, and underneath I could clearly see that he was wearing a bright yellow Safe-T-Guard Jockstrap. The twink slid the pants down off of the bear's hips; they slid down to his ankles. The bear's legs were thick, hairy and very muscular. It was obvious that this massive piece of manpower spent a great deal of time working out. His man scent was so strong that I could smell it through the glory hole as it filled the entire booth that he and the twink were in.

The twink started to kiss and lick the pouch of the big man, "Hell yeah boy, get after it, make me feel that you are worthy of getting with a real man like me. Suck that fucking pouch clean, get all those fucking rank ass man stains off of it." He said as he continued to caress the back of the young blonde's head. The twink started to suck on the elastic mesh pouch of the jock. I was sure that he was finding his mouth being filled with a wide variety of tastes at the moment, and I found myself envious. I was sure that a man like that surely had a bit of dried cum, a few piss stains, a pretty generous amount of sweat and more in the pouch of that jock. I only wished I had been faster and had gotten to him first, but then the hard cock that I felt in the front of my khakis at the moment meant that even though I was not the lucky guy who had the opportunity to worship the massive bear stud, I was still going to be able to enjoy the show of him using the prissy twink that was on his knees in front of him.

"Oh yeah, boy get that pouch nice and clean for me." The bear said to the other man. He pushed the face of the twink harder into the pouch of the jock. The twink sucked harder and harder as he tried his best to do what the dominate man told him to and suck every last stain for the jock pouch. I could see that the bear's big man meat was starting to swell and stretch the mesh jock pouch. The contents of the pouch were already substantial to begin with, but now, that pouch was getting a work out of its own.

"You ready to eat my meat boy?" The bear asked.

"Yes sir," the twink said.

"Then ask me for it boy, beg me to suck my fucking cock," the bear said.

"Please sir, please let me suck your cock."

"No way boy, you ain't begging hard enough; show me that you want my big meat, be a good little slut and beg me for my chub of bear steak bitch" the bear said.

"Please sir, please big bear. I need your meat, please let me suck your cock, please sir, please," the twink begged the big bear as he massaged the pouch of the big man's jock with both of his hands. The bear just smiled and pulled the jock pouch aside. His thick 7-inch cock came into view, and I almost creamed off in my own tighty-whities when I saw it sticking out form his thick furry bush. Behind it hung a massive set of low-hanging balls that were the size of large chicken eggs. His cock was uncut and his foreskin was stretched tight over his large shiny purple head. The twink took in a deep breath and looked on with as much awe at the big man's fuck pole as I had. The twink looked up at the bear that just looked down at him and smiled.

"You wanted it boy, get after it, I ain't got all day!" He said and the twink didn't need a second invitation. He took the big bears cock into his hand and pulled the foreskin the rest of the way back. He stuck out his tongue and started to lick the large glands of the burly stud. The bear took in a deep breath and let his head tilt back with his eyes closed as he felt the incredible sensation of the twink sucking on his big stalk of pride flesh.

"God damn boy, that feels fucking awesome." He said as he let his hand once again find its way to the back of the twink's head. The smaller man licked the end of the brute's cock as if it was an ice-cream cone. I moved my hands down to the front of my own pants, unfastened my belt and opened my fly. My thick nine inches was rock hard in my underwear. I pulled the front of my tighty-whities down and let my tightly circumcised cock come out to play. It didn't take long for my knob and hand to be coated with a thick layer of my slimy precum. I have always been a heavy leaker, but since I'm a total bottom (with the exception of a few very choice encounters where I decided to see how the top half lived), most of my fuck lube ends up either in the front of my own undershorts or dripping down to the carpet while I have a big and burly plug in my ass with his half a pound of tube steak. Right now, it was providing more than enough lube for me to slide my gripping hand up and down my shaft as I watched the burly blue collar stud in the next booth get his man stick mouth polished by the skinny blond cum slut that he found himself with the opportunity to use.

"Oh fuck yeah, that's nice boy, get down there on it, real low, get all the way to the base," the bear said. That's exactly what the twink was determined to do; he had already managed to get more than half of the big man's cock into his mouth and had even managed to take the head past his throat opening without gagging. I had to admit that I was impressed by that; I might have to ask the kid for pointers on how to swallow a sword as well as he did.

The bear was growing impatient though and he wanted all of it down the guy's gullet now! He grabbed the back of the kids head and started to push it down his shaft. The kid choked a little but soon caught up. The bear continued his power slide deep into the guy's mouth, and soon he had gotten what he wanted. He had the face of the twink buried in his bush, the waistband do his jockstrap pressing against the forehead of the smaller younger man. After a few moments of savoring the pleasure of being 7 inches deep into the guy's throat, the bear let up on the pressure and the twink's head slid half way up his shaft once more. The twink had gotten proof of his ability to take the long thick meat staff now and he was gonna do it again. He did, over and over. He went to the base of the bears cock and came back up to the tip. Soon, the bear was back in charge though, grabbing the sides of the twink's head and starting in on a full-fledged throat fuck that continued for several minutes before the bear pulled the guy's head form his groin and tilted it back.

"You wanna get fucked by the big meat boy?"

"Yes sir, please," the twink said as he started to stand up.

"I don't play safe, you up for that? You want me, you got to go bareback," the bear said.

"Anything sir, just please fuck me, now please!" the twink said. The bear smiled and turned him around. He planted him hard against the wall. He reached around and unfastened the belt of the twink. His pants were loose, and the bear was able to yank them down to his ankles in one move without even unbuttoning them. He looked at the bright pink bikini briefs that the twink was wearing and laughed.

"I like the drawer's boy. I think they fit your pussy ass just right. I can't fuck you through them though, or then again maybe I can punk!" the bear said as he grabbed the center of the bikini briefs ass and ripped a large hole in the middle of the fabric. The twink let out a moan as the bear made the opening that he would fuck him through. Soon, he felt the end of the bears cock against the tight pucker of his hole. My hand was still working on my rod as I wished to myself how much I really wanted that twink to be me. I wanted to feel that heavy piece of hard man meat pressing against my tight ass hole. I loved to take it up the ass, the bigger the better and it had been so long. I wanted that big stud to be using me right now. The bear leaned back and spat on the end of his cock as he nestled it against the boy's sphincter.

"Get ready boy, here I..." he gave a hard

shove before he could finish the sentence, the boy let out a gasp, "come!" he started to laugh as he pressed hard and the whole of his cock slid deep into the boys ass hole uncovered from any condom. I wondered what the status of the bear was. Did the twink even think about what the risks were that he was taking right then, letting a big man like that fuck him up the ass unprotected, a man he didn't even know. I thought about it and I found it hot. I love to bareback, but I only do it with guys that I know are safe and clean, never with a stranger, well almost never. I could be persuaded to make an exception with a guy like that though. The bear pushed hard until he felt his large hairy balls slap against the back of the twink's own sack. He pulled back just enough to get a stroke going and then slammed back in. Over and over, he drove in and out of the twink's hole. He was fucking him so hard that the force of the action was making the booth partition shake. He reached up and put his hand on the shoulder of the twink. He was giving him all he had to give him now. Grunting and groaning, fucking him hard and deep, giving him what he had wanted, what he knew he would be getting since the very moment that he had walked into the booth with the bear standing there rubbing the crotch of his camo pants.

"I'm about to cum, boy, I'm gonna shoot this shit straight up your ass with no rubber, you like hearing that?" The bear asked grunting the question out as he hard fucked the twink.

"Yes sir, please, dump it in me. I don't care about the risk, I need your seed inside of me, please big bear, please breed me hard, please!" the twink cried out as he shot off his load into the front of his pink bikini briefs. The fabric turned dark pink were his own load of semen had soaked in. My own balls were tightening up now. The bear drove in to the hilt and grunted. He was shooting, he was spraying his questionable load up inside of the twink's ass, and the twink was shaking as he felt the powerful blast of hot liquid course though his insides. My own load shot out of my cock and splattered on the partition wall. Rope after rope of my own sticky sperm coated the wall and started to run down in a slimy mass. I felt weak and breathless.

I watched through the hole as the bear pulled his cock out of the twink's hole and stepped back spreading the cheeks of the young man and smiled as he saw the first dribbles of his man gravy start to drip out of the guys ass and his now well-opened ass hole. The bears cum dripped out onto the floor of the booth in a long stream as the bear continued to hold his hand on the back of the twink to keep him in place. He stroked his softening meat as he watched his load run out and collect on the floor. When he had seen enough, he moved up and whispered something to the twink that I could not hear, the twink looked relived. I could only assume that he had just informed him of his STD status, but I could not be sure of that. He moved his jock back over his hairy heavy manhood and pulled his pants up fastening them and his belt before he turned and walked out of the booth. A few minutes later, after I had put myself back into my own briefs and zipped up the twink pulled his pants up and left, a small cum stain started to form on the back of his pants.

When both men were gone, I went into the booth and got a good look at the huge load of thick white cum that had dripped out of the twink's hole onto the floor. I knelt down and stuck my finger into it. It was creamy, rich, and I could tell it was filled with millions and millions of sperm. This was the cum of a man who was very fertile, and I only wished it wasn't wasted on the dirty floor but rather in my ass or stomach where it belonged. I looked over as I was about to stand and saw the wallet of the bear lying under the small bench on the booth. I picked it up and opened it. There was a lot of cash, a few credit cards, an STD testing card and his ID. I looked at the ID. His name was Jerry Holbrook. I had his address and his University ID. He worked for the engineer and maintenance department. I would give him a call and let him know I had the wallet. I was tempted to look at the STD card and find out the status but I didn't. I closed up the wallet and stood. Just as I was about to leave the booth, the big bear came back in. "Oh hi, I think that's my wallet, must had slid out when I was...well yeah," he said, "so did you enjoy the show, dude?" He asked.

"You knew?" I said

"Yeah, I saw you through the glory hole watching," I handed him the wallet.

"I was just about to call you and let you know you dropped this, I am the manager of the store," I said.

"Oh well thanks, nice place you got here."

"Thanks," I said. He reached for his belt and started to unbuckle it.

"You want me to tell you what I told the little punk I just bred after I shot my load up his ass without a rubber?" He said as he opened his pants and exposed the front of the yellow Safe-T-Guard Jockstrap underneath.

"Sure," I said.

"I told him what that little card in my wallet says. Did you look at the card boy?" It had been a longtime since a big and burly blue-collar bear stud called me boy.

"I saw it but I didn't look, it's none of my business what it says. That's strictly your business, and if you want someone to know, then you should be the one to tell them, right?" I responded.

"Oh I think you didn't look because you didn't really want to know; you'd like to keep that part of what you saw hotter by not knowing the truth." He said as he slid his pants down his legs once more. I looked down at his jockstrap pouch and my breath started to get short again, my pulse started to get fast and my knees started to get weak. He moved his hands to the pouch and started to massage himself. "Don't worry, boy, I'll tell you what the card says. The only thing I want to know is, do you want me to tell you now or after I shoot the next huge load of my thick, creamy could-be, could be-not, ball snot up your shitter and grind it into the walls of your rectum? Which is it boy, you want to spin the wheel of luck and ride my fat fuck rod knowing or not knowing your fate, cause we both know you're gonna ride it either way?" The bear said as he pulled the pouch aside, and I saw that his cock was once again starting to rise up from his hairy salt and peppered bush.

"After big bear. After..." I said as I lowered myself to my knees in front of him.

7 VAMPIRE STRIPPERS FROM HELL PART 1

Made

My life as a vampire has not been a long one; it has only been a little more than a century, yet I still remember the day that I was made as if it were yesterday. I will never forget the feel of the fangs as they fed on me and changed my life forever. Back then, it was common for a person to be a victim of a vampire, especially females, as women in those days were weaker and more timid. My experiences with vampires go beyond the one that I had personally; in fact, my first encounter with a vampire was actually with my sister. She was young back then and was very trusting of people, this trust of people would be how she would soon become a victim. My sister was a beautiful young lady. She has long red hair and the most piercing green eyes. To any man who saw her, she appeared to be quite a catch as her beauty included her perfectly shaped body. Her heaving breasts protruded from her clothes as two perfectly molded mounds of flesh. The perfection continued all the way down to her perfect ass. I must admit, even, I was turned on at times by my sister.

I always knew that at some point in my life that I would have to face this. It became apparent when my sister was made. That moment led me to feel that I would soon be joining the creatures of the night, become one of them with or without my permission. But, before we get to my story, it is important that you know about what happened to my sister. This will help you to better understand the events that were set into motion with a single night all those years ago.

This is her story.

Tracy Anne Madison was considered to be the ideal student at Mount Holyoke College while she was in attendance in 1890. There was not one student that had such perfect marks and no one was as well behaved as she. She did not look on any kind of fun as acceptable. We came from a near perfect home. The only blemish on our reputation was the fact that our mother had disappeared a few years prior when we were still just little girls. Many people were of the opinion that our mother had been killed by some marauding stranger while others believed that she had been so unhappy in her loveless marriage to our business obsessed father she had run off to Europe with another love who held her true heart. Still other rumors stated that she had decided to live a life of decadence and depravity and had become one of the many ladies of the night who offered the men of the factories around Boston a good time when they left work for the day. The actual whereabouts our mother was a mystery but our father raised us both as good girls. He taught us the values that we needed and provided us with an education, despite the fact that it was frowned upon for girls to be educated in those days.

With all of that against her, she studied hard and tried to get the best marks she could. All through school, she had suffered a great amount of teasing and ridicule from both professors as well as students. Our father had a good name and possessed great influence in New York at that time; the fact that our mother had disappeared as she did was well known.

My sister's dedication to school was looked at as being that of brown nosing by her classmates.

The truth of the matter was that she found the cold, measured, and stable world of Academia to be the place that she could escape to and attain peace and comfort that she could not find elsewhere.

After graduation, she was accepted into Holyoke in southern Massachusetts. Our overprotective father would have preferred she attended Vassar, but she was insistent. She wanted to attend Holyoke to be with her only real friend on the world, Maggie Swift, who had started at that school the previous year. Tracy soon became the brightest student in Anne-Marie Lachaussee's World History class. It was not uncommon for Mrs. Lachaussee to ask Tracy to stay and help her with a number of different projects. One afternoon, there was major storm moved in and it was raining very heavily. Mrs. Lachaussee offered to escort Tracy back to the Girl's Dormitory but first she needed Tracy help her grade some term papers. Tracy saw nothing wrong with this as she was used to helping Mrs. Lachaussee. While most of the work took place in the classroom, Tracy saw nothing wrong with helping her out at her home, which was just outside the walls of the campus. A few hours passed and the women were talking and reviewing the papers while outside the storm was not letting up.

"Why not just spend the night here dear? It's monstrous out there."

Mrs. Lachaussee offered with a smile on her face. Little did Tracey know that the smile she was seeing had an evil agenda behind it, and that the kind, sweet professor that she had grown so fond of had plans for the evening; plans that would change my sister's life forever.

Later that night Tracy was asleep in the guest room. A breeze entered the space. Tracy was awoken by this but did not see anything in the room with her despite the fact that she could feel a presence in the room.

"Probably just my imagination" she thought.

She fell back asleep quickly. Thirty minutes later Tracy was awoken yet again by another breeze. This time she felt a hand working its way up her inner leg. Tracy awoke to see Mrs. Lachaussee standing over her rubbing the inside of Tracy's leg under the fabric of her nightgown. Tracy was frozen. She did not know what to do at that moment. Her first instinct was to try to run away, but she felt a paralyzing fear that was holding her down.

"Mrs. Lachaussee what are you doing?"

"Relax, Tracy, this is what is best for

you, your sweet legs, your perfect skin and your round bosom. You will make an excellent apprentice for my skills to be carried on through."

Tracy was rather confused as to what Mrs. Lachaussee was talking about, what skills, what apprenticeship?

There was another sensation that was taking control of her. She was experiencing a new feeling at the sight of the naked form of Mrs. Lachaussee. Her full, perfect breasts and the milky tone of her skin, which led down to her perfectly shaved bush made Tracy, get a burning that was deep in the recess of her cunt.

Mrs. Lachaussee bent over and slid her hand under the neck of Tracy's gown. She felt Tracy's nipples in her hands, and gave a gentle tug. This caused Tracy to feel a bolt of electrical current shoot down her body and right into her pussy. Tracy had never been with a man, let alone a woman. She was saving herself for that special someone and had never even played with her pussy as this was looked upon as a sin.

Here she was now; her History teacher bent over her tugging on her nipples like there was no tomorrow. While Tracy was experiencing this sensation in her nipples, Mrs. Lachaussee took her hand and lightly started to massage the younger girl's tender vagina. The touch was alarming and caused Tracy to jolt back on the bed.

"Take your nightgown off, girl."

Tracy did what she was told without question, it was almost as if she were under a spell cast by Mrs. Lachaussee. Tracy sat up and removed her gown. Her full breasts protruded out as she arched her back. She was now lying there, naked, before her teacher who was somehow commanding her very will.

"Come with me. I want to show you something very special."

Doing as she was told, she followed the teacher into her own bedroom where she was told to lay on her back on the bed. Getting into the middle of the bed, Tracy did as she was told. Mrs. Lachaussee got onto the bed and began to make her way into a position to straddle Tracy. Placing her snatch in Tracy's face, she gave the command,

"Eat it girl, Lick my womanhood, dear."

Tracy was not sure what to do. Her instinct was to do as she had been commanded. Tracy took her tongue and gave the wet twat a little of a lick.

"Take your tongue, girl, and slide it into my hole, dear, don't be afraid, do it now!"

Tracy locked eyes with Mrs. Lachaussee and was overtaken by an uncontrollable appetite to have the teacher's cunt in her mouth. With a passion that Tracy never knew she had, she began to work over the teacher's pussy with purpose.

"There you go, girl, drink up all of my juices. You like to have my womanhood in your face being made to lick my juices up like a dog with a water bowl, don't you?"

"Yes Ma'am, I love the smell of your cherry blossom. It is intoxicating to my senses,"

By now, she was able to feel her own cunt begin to pour out her own juices. Mrs. Lachaussee must have picked up on Tracy's scent as she reached behind her and began to play with Tracy's pussy from behind. She soon began to drive a couple of fingers into Tracy's eagerly awaiting hole.

"You like to have your hole played with don't you girl?"

"Yes Ma'am, I love it," Tracey admitted but she did not know why

Mrs. Lachaussee got even more excited hearing this and it sent a gush of juices shooting from her hole into Tracy's face. The smell of Mrs. Lachaussee's wet cunt was more than just intoxicating. For the first time in her life, Tracy felt alive. It was almost as if Tracy was possessed by a sexual spirit that was intent on getting the goddess of a woman in front of her to have a mind-blowing orgasm, as if it was the last thing that she was going to do.

The feelings that her teacher's fingers were awakening in her made Tracy feel more alive than she ever had. A number of the sensations that she was feeling caused her to arch her back in an effort to drive the fingers deeper into her hot, wet, love tunnel. The arching of her back also allowed for her eagerly awaiting tits to beg for attention to her flesh mounds that were standing straight up begging for a little attention.

"Eat my mound harder girl; make me feel that you are living just for my pleasure alone."

Being spoken to like a dirty whore was actually exciting her and was causing her to become wet between her legs. All she wanted was for Mrs. Lachaussee to drive her fingers into her wet pussy and cause her to erupt in a mind-blowing orgasm.

"Finger my pussy; make me feel like a cheap prostitute, I want to feel your fingers drive me into an orgasmic fit."

Mrs. Lachaussee withdrew her fingers from Tracy's snatch and took a lick of the sweet nectar that oozed from Tracy's hole.

"My love, you will get what you desire soon enough. Now you are to focus on giving your mistress the pleasure that she deserves."

When Tracy heard this, her eyes shot up to the woman that was straddled over her face, and that is when she saw the two fangs sticking out.

"My God, I'm in bed with a vampire,"

Tracy thought to herself. The thought of the situation she was in sent bolts of excitement through her body as well as sending fear through her veins. A lot of the behavior that Mrs. Lachaussee exhibited all made sense now as Tracy placed all the pieces of the puzzle together.

"Now eat my vagina out and make me orgasm girl, I am getting impatient and I do not like for my orgasms to be delayed."

This time she drove her fingers deep into Tracy's pussy and made her almost wince in pain. This led to her feeling like a woman possessed and sent chills down her spine. Without notice, Mrs. Lachaussee dismounted her prey and went to her nightstand drawer where she pulled out a double-ended phallus made of carved wood and inlaid with bone. She shoved it deep inside her.

"Let me show you the joys of having a good fuck, my dear."

Mrs. Lachaussee quickly took the other end and shoved it deep into Tracy's wet, eagerly awaiting pussy. The feel of this being shoved into her almost made her orgasm instantly.

"No, no my little girl, you will not orgasm before your mistress, I forbid it, it's not respectful." Her tone was a lot more relaxed than and not as aggressive as it had been. The sight of her teacher fucking her with the large dildo sent waves of pleasure through her body. Then Mrs. Lachaussee began to work the dildo into both of them

"Play with your nipples, girl, take your fingers and twist your fleshy nipples, make your mistress happy and please her while you work over your tits."

Tracy did as she was told placing one of her nipples in between a couple of fingers and giving it a slight little twist. The feeling of this sent electrical charges through her body and the result was a little river of wetness that oozed out of her tight pink hole.

"Yes, girl, please you. Lick your nipples and dig your fingernails into the flesh of your perky round flesh mounds. I want to see you dig your nails in while licking your pink untouched nipples. How does it make you feel that the first person to take that tight hole is your history teacher with her large wooden phallus? Knowing that regardless of how many men that you will have make relations with you, your mistress will be the first to taste your juices as well as enter your tight wet hole?"

At that moment, Mrs. Lachaussee let out a massive howl as well as a gush of pussy juices that was like a fire hose had gone off. The look of pleasure was more than apparent in the face of Mrs. Lachaussee as well as in Tracy's face. Tracy was more concerned with the woman in front of her getting pleasure than she was in getting her own.

"Now my little girl, you are more than welcome to pleasure yourself. Let me help you."

Mrs. Lachaussee went up and began to lick her.

"God, girl, you taste wonderful. I have had a lot of women before me, but you have the tastiest womanhood I have ever enjoyed. I love the way that your hole eagerly offers up its sweet nectar for its mistress to lick up."

Tracy was more than eager to have her pussy eaten as this was the first time that she had even felt any type of this pleasure.

"My girl, you will be a great sex partner for the rest of the men that you will encounter for me. I have a special task for you. After tonight, your life will take on a new meaning and you will become one of us, the people that live for the dark. Why do you think that I have night classes? It is because of the sun, my girl; you will soon learn that the sun will be your enemy and all of the joys that can be had when you feed on a person."

With that, Mrs. Lachaussee drove her head down into her pubic mound and gave a bite to her pussy lips. There was a mixture of pain and pleasure that shot through Tracy's body. There was a feeling like nothing she had ever felt before going through her. It was as if a person had turned on her sexual appetite button and she was in full force.

The sensation of the fangs being driven into her cunt was sending waves of pleasure throughout her body, the sucking of her lips as the blood was funneled out of her drove her sexual appetite into overdrive. The feel of the fangs driving into Tracy's lips, caused her clit to quiver out of control. This sensation alone was enough to make her cum instantly. Deeper she drove her fangs into Tracy's wet pussy, and this was just what Tracy needed to bring her out of her repressed state. She lost all control of her senses and began to moan in a loud voice.

"OHHH yes Mistress Ann-Marie, feed off of my tender lips, make me feel your power and take me as yours. I live to swerve you and will do anything you want or desire. Keep feeding off of me and make me orgasm for you, I want to orgasm for you so you can taste all of my essence and see that I am more than a perfect servant for you."

Tracy grabbed the back of Ann-Marie Lachaussee's head and began to drive her pussy into her mistress's face, with each ounce of aggression that Tracy showed, the harder and more intense that Anne-Marie fed off the young college student. Anne Marie came up off Tracy's pussy, took the dildo, and shoved it into the wet hole

"My dear, it is not for me to make you orgasm, you have to make that happen, I will gladly lick your juices, but you must be the one that actually makes yourself orgasm."

With this Tracy began to work the dildo into her cunt with a force that she had never known was in her. The in and out motion of the dildo hitting her G-spot, had her on the verge of having her first orgasm. Tracy could feel the intense event building and wanted nothing more than to please her mistress. It was then that she, with all of the energy she could gather, let out an orgasm that sent waves of energy shooting through her body and a gush of fluid spewing from her cunt, Anne-Marie enjoyed the sight and licked the fluids up eagerly.

"You and I are now one my sweet, I am your mistress, and you are to be my servant. Your job will be to find more men and women to feed off as well as bringing me more to feed off of. The difference between us and the rest of the traditional vampires is that we feed off of sex; the pure passion that we experience in sex, is what we feed off. I, for example, fed off the juices from your pussy and got my energy from your orgasm. Now go and rest for the night, you will need your energy for your first task tomorrow night. This will be the true test of your powers as you will need to find a man upon which you will be able to feed off."

Tracy went to sleep for the rest of the night as well as all of the next day. I did not hear anything from my sister for three months.

One evening, I was walking through the street of the city and heard someone call my name. I turned and saw my sister, whom we had all given up for dead, coming out of the shadows of a doorway. I was overjoyed and rushed to her. We spoke briefly and she explained to me that she would have to go away and that she may never see me again. She told me that it was best to let father believe that she was dead, for in a way, she was. It was many years until I saw her again. When I did, things would be very different for me, and I would have long since understood what had happened to her.

So here I sit waiting for my train to a new city, I have a job at one of the strip clubs in Vegas as a dancer. I am starting a new volume of the diary that I have kept for over 140 years, since the days I was a little girl in New York City. I actually would love to tell the world all about the fun that I am about to have, as a stripper in Vegas working the night shift, but that is not possible. Till the day that it is, I will simply record the life that I live. Yes, this new chapter of my life is sure to be fun. Vegas is a fun place, so let the fun, and the feeding, begin.

8 VAMPIRE STRIPPERS FROM HELL PART 2

Memories

Life in Las Vegas is a far cry from the life I have been used to. I grew up in New York City and had not seen a city quite like Las Vegas; all of the neon lights and the hustle and bustle of the people coming and going is overwhelming.

I thought about all I have seen in all of my 140 years on the earth. I have seen the entire era of Ellis Island. I have seen the dedication of the Statue of Liberty and a great number of things in the city that never sleeps. I recently moved to Las Vegas from New York City where I worked as a stripper at one of the premiere strip clubs in the city. While I cannot drop any names, I will say that the name rhymes with" buster".

There I was making a good living shaking my ass and making men every night go home wanting to cream their underwear just for a taste of my sweet cherry pie. Their wives should have thanked me; I was doing them a favor by giving their husbands something to fantasize about when they were fucking their wives. Although I have been alive for around 140 years, I still have the complexion of a twenty-one year old. You could say that I have really good genes. I have not even been in the city a week, and I already have men that request me when they come into the club I where I perform. I am the newest performer at the Broken Bone strip club.

Having the whole vampire issue to contend with, I have had to hire a new assistant out here in Vegas. That whole sun, daylight thing can really screw up a vampire's life. My old assistant chose to not leave New York City, because he wanted to pursue a career in theater. I personally think being an usher at a movie theater is a low expectation to have, but who am I to judge?

I met my new assistant at the club. He is named Darren, and he is a dream of a man. I could not ask for a better man to take care of my every need. While he is a little confused about the reasons why I am not able to head out into the sun, he does what I ask and in return, he has a free place to live. There are other advantages that come from this arrangement as well; one advantage is having a man around that can fix the items that a delicate flower of a female such as myself shouldn't have to deal with.

I have wanted to fuck Darren from the moment I laid eyes on him, but knew it would just complicate things. One night I let my guard down and what happened could only be described as pure enjoyment. I wish that Darren could have remembered this, more about that as I go along. I considered this one of the most intense sexual adventures that I have had since arriving in Las Vegas.

It all started about a month ago on a Saturday night. Darren and I were both scheduled to work the night shift. Since Darren is one of the bouncers, I feel safe in his hands if any shit was going to go down. Darren and I had a system; he would know if I needed him right away, even without my saying anything. If a customer was getting a little frisky, and I was okay with the situation, I would tug on my left nipple. If things were getting out of hand, then I would squeeze my right breast hard. This was Darren's sign to come and remove the asshole from the situation. At 6'6 and 280lbs, Darren has little to no trouble in helping young men to see the error in their ways.

I had a customer that had paid for two-for-one lap dances. At first, all was going well, but by the middle of the first song, he began to get a little out of bounds. Trying to be professional, I tried to discourage him from his actions. A couple of moments later, he slipped his hands down my G-string and tried to begin to finger my pussy. Normally I would love a man fingering my pussy, but a drunken, retired Marine was not my cup of tea. I asked him to stop and was met with a hearty slap to the face. Darren was on it like lighting, He grabbed me and got me out of the way, then proceeded to lift the drunken individual out of his seat and drag him to the front door. It was moments like that watching Darren get physical with an individual made me get wet in my panties. The rest of the night went on and I had little to no trouble at all. I had a couple of issues that needed to be dealt with, but I was able to handle them. At the end of the night, I was in the dressing room changing to get ready to go home. Darren was coming through doing his usual rounds of making sure that all was well and no customers were hiding in the dressing rooms. I noticed him stop and just look at me while I was changing. I admit I have a hot body; it's good genes.

"Are you checking me out Darren? I see you standing there and watching me change. You enjoy watching me every night up on the stage dancing and gyrating, I bet you would love to be that pole as I slide up and down on it all night long. I bet you get hard every time I place my twat in a guy's face for him to get a hearty sniff. You would love to sniff my pussy as I grind it in your face wouldn't you?"

"Look, Angela, I think you are awesome and a great person. I have no problem being your "Assistant" and doing the things that need to be done because of your issues with the sun. I admit, you have a remarkable body and any guy would be lucky to fuck you, but I do not want sex to ruin the relationship that we have. I feel that we can be great friends even with the sexual tension that we both have. I will continue doing what I always have which is to watch you at night and then masturbate while thinking about you, which makes things a lot less complicated."

"Darren, let's go grab some breakfast, It's been a hell of a night for the two of us."

Darren and I went to the nearby IHOP and enjoyed a stack of never ending pancakes each. After we were finally done, we decided to head back to the apartment and sit around just talking and watching television that we recorded the night before. I enjoy the time we spent together, but was secretly hoping that one day, he would make a move on me. Then I could follow up on it and give him what we both secretly wanted. We sat there watching television curled up with one another until we both fell asleep. Darren's hand made its way up to my breast and he cupped it. He was out cold and had no idea what he was doing; it must have been the Jack Daniels that we were drinking that had taken its effect on him.

I helped Darren to his room and helped to get him undressed. It would have been a more difficult task as if it had not been for my remarkable strength from being a vampire. I would have failed at getting him undressed. I got him stripped all the way down and he fell onto his back on the bed. Sticking up from his hairy crotch was an 8.5" rock hard cock that was just begging to have a pussy wrapped around it. I have watched him and his girlfriend when they fucked, while they never knew I was there. I saw every time he shoved that meat slab deep into her pussy. I desperately wanted to be her and feel his rod slamming into my cunt while I begged him to fuck me harder. Here I was with the golden ring in front of me, all I had to do was squat down over it, and I could fulfill my desperate need. That would possibly cause trouble between us and I did enjoy his company. I enjoyed our hours just sitting around and laughing. All of that could be lost with one night of passion. Because of the risk, I had to try and pass and not be tempted by the cock that looked at me and swelled at the mere thought of invading my hole.

I then lost all self-control and took the plunge; I stripped off my shirt and shorts and made quick work of getting my bra and panties off. I straddled Darren and placed my cunt right under his nose. As if on autopilot, he grabbed my hips and brought me closer to his face, his tongue met the top of my clit and suddenly the sexual tension between us seemed to break, as he quickly went to work on my clit playing with it with his tongue.

Every time that he took a lick, I was sent into an ecstasy overload. I then buried my cunt as deep into his face as I could. I wanted him to get the full experience of my pussy; I was a master of giving a man a taste of my snatch and tonight, Darren was getting the full course meal with the free dessert as well. Even in his drunken state, he showed that he was well versed at the art of cunnilingus. The feel of his tongue hitting my G-spot was driving me into frenzy. I guess all of the excitement from tonight had built up as this had me on edge ready to explode at a moment's notice. My pussy was beginning to quiver. I was enjoying the movements of his tongue, but I was not the type to be greedy, I was determined that I was going to give him some type of pleasure no matter what. I quickly removed my snatch from his face and did what was probably the one thing that we had both wanted me to do.

I straddled his very rigid and rock hard member and with as much ease as I could muster, lowered myself down onto it. This sent waves of pleasure throughout my body. The feel of his prick inside of me was exhilarating and I never wanted it to stop. I was determined for one thing and that was I was going to ride his pole until he shot a thick creamy load off into my eagerly awaiting hole. I had to admit, I was turned on by the thought of fucking a guy who was drunk and unable to know what was going on. The thought had me all wet with anticipation of the moment. I thought there were a number of issues that need to be addressed when it came to the situation that was unfolding, and the main one was what this would do to our relationship. I was his roommate as well as a co-worker.

"You like having that pussy of yours fucked, don't you?"

The question startled me. I had no idea as to if it was Darren or if it was it the alcohol that was talking. Regardless, I was in a weird situation, as I had to wonder if this was going to be something that he would remember in the morning. Regardless of the fallout, I had come this far, there was no point in turning back now; I had to just finish what I started. I continued to ride up and down on his rigid member feeling as it probed deeper into me with each and every thrust. I enjoyed being on top as it allowed me to get into the position that best fit me and my needs. I was able to control the rhythm and speed.

I wanted to scream out for Darren to fuck me harder, but I knew that might shake him fully awake from his drunken state and I could not risk that. I could feel his shaft growing in girth inside my hole, the feeling of his hard prick inside me gave me a full feeling that I enjoyed a lot. The tip of his knob was tickling the inner walls of my pussy on each down stroke that I took. I could not take it anymore, I had to just release all of my energy and let the world know that I was enjoying the fucking that I was getting.

"There you go big man, fuck my hole, slide that large member of your in and out in me. I want to feel the length of your shaft going in and out of me. Fuck me, fuck me, fuck my fucking pussy like I know you have wanted to do ever since you laid eyes on me and saw me naked. Take my nipples and twist them as hard as you can. Take me and ravish my young body."

I had become unhinged, I was truly an animal in bed, and I liked the way it felt to have a man as powerful as Darren fucking me. I was turned on by the thought of those men who all wanted to take me home and fuck me but would never get the chance. Here was Darren, who every time he got the chance, saw me naked. I remember all the times since he moved in that I masturbated thinking about his cock in me. Now here I was, my pussy soaking with juices, as it was the first time in a long time I was able to let myself go. If Darren remembered or not I did not care, all I was interested in was this hunk of a man deep inside my hole fucking me like there was no tomorrow.

Darren had begun to stir and was beginning to take control as he began bouncing me up and down on the length of his shaft. I began to believe that he had been awake for the entire thing and wanted to see if I was going to make a move or not.

"Come, Angela, ride my cock, you know you have wanted this as much as I have. Come on baby and let loose on me, let me feel your pussy lips grab onto my prick and hold onto it. I want you to cum hard, I want you to have an orgasm like you have never had before. Come on baby and cum with me you fucking sexy bitch."

I had to admit the talking dirty to me was actually getting me off. I enjoyed when a guy would call me a slut, whore, bitch or anything else that they could come up with. This along with the fact I had wanted to fuck the shit out of Darren, this all led to me letting out one of the most mind blowing orgasms I had had in a long time. The feel of all my sexual energy being released made me feel like I had never felt before.

Darren pushed me back onto the bed and spread my legs. He had not cum yet and was eager to lick my love juices up even more than before. He carefully made his way around my pussy making sure to lick every area that my juices had reached. This made me come close to having another release.

Darren straddled me and slid his wet cock into my mouth, the taste of my own juices on his prick caused me to begin to passionately finger fuck my snatch. I was getting off on the way that he was treating me by taking my head and bobbing it up and down on his tool.

"Come on, bitch you want me to fucking cum in you don't you. I bet you would love it if I took this cock, shoved it down your throat, and released my jizz. That is not going to happen, as I have a better place to plant it instead."

Darren took his cock out of my mouth and aimed it directly at my large tits. I knew I was about to get a load of hot, thick cum all over my tits. With one hand I reached up and gave my left nipple a tug, it was moments later that he released one of the largest loads a man had released on me in quite a long while. The feel of his hot man juice splashing and sticking to my large tits sent me into frenzy and I had another orgasm while I was finger fucking my pussy. This made Darren smile as he licked every drop.

After the mind-blowing sex I had just had, I needed a cigarette badly. I allowed the smoke to linger so I could enjoy it as much as I was enjoying the sensation of a very successful fuck. I needed a shower and knew that Darren would try to sneak and watch. I went to the bathroom and started the water for my shower. Stepping in, I left the curtain open for Darren to come and watch. Why stop now? I did my usual routine of masturbating to the thought of Darren. This time I was able to become a lot wet than I had ever before as

I thought about the two of us as we fucked our brains out. As I hoped he would, Darren came in and watched me, stroking his long pole, and it made me get even wetter. I finished cleaning up and stepped out to dry off and head to bed. It had been a long night and an exhausting one for the both of us. I walked over to Darren and looked deep into his eyes. I knew that the only way that I was going to get out of this situation was to use a mind control trick that some vampires have called Glamoring someone. This in essence allows the vampire to control the mind of their subject and make the subject believe whatever the vampire wants them to believe.

I looked Darren deep into his eyes and focused my thoughts toward one single thought.

"Darren, this was just a dream, me and you did not just fuck our brains out and have the most mind blowing sex we had ever had."

I hated to do that, and knew that Darren would kill me if he ever found out I glamored him for my own needs. It was fun knowing that all I had to do was glamor him and we could fuck. The odd part was, deep down I felt bad for doing this and really did not know how to deal with it. I was only used to Glamoring a person if they discovered what I was and threatened to tell someone about me. I had never used it in regards to getting sex out of the deal.

I got up the next morning and surprised Darren with a full layout of Chinese food; this was something that was reserved for only special occasions.

"What's up sleepy head, sleep well?"

"What's with the Chinese food, what is going on?"

"Nothing special. I just thought we had not had Chinese in a long while and thought it would be nice for a change. I will admit I have a hell of a hangover. I need to lay off the Jack Daniels and not get so smashed. Besides, today marks two months since we moved in together, why don't we rent a couple of movies and just take today to relax and unwind?"

Darren responded, "I had the wildest dream last night, I dreamt that me and you had the wildest sex. It all seemed so real. I must have enjoyed it as my sheets were crusted over. I must have had a wet dream. I hope you are not offended, I guess it was just what we were talking about last night somehow made its way into my dream. It was so real I swear when I got up this morning I could smell you on my sheets."

"Wow you must have really been charged up in regards to thinking about me and you actually having sex. Normally

I would be offended, but I actually am a little flattered that I left that much of an impression on you. Who knows maybe one day me and you will get the chance to sleep together and it not ruin our relationship. For the moment just enjoy the Chinese spread that I had delivered. I am so glad that Kim Chi is right down the street. Henry makes the best Szechuan pork this side of the Vegas strip."

The rest of the day, we sat around just talking and getting to know one another a lot better. I was amazed at learning that Darren played football in college and that due to a slight misstep, which his football career was cut short when he fractured his knee. That is when he decided to take a job being a bouncer, as he was able to do that without too much trouble and effort. He had come to Vegas one weekend to take a chance at the casino, met a girl named Tracy-Ann who suggested that they get married. Darren was left standing at the altar empty handed. His wallet had been stolen, and all of his credit cards maxed out.

He went from club to club placing applications in to find a place that would hire him. It was only after walking into the Broken Bone strip club when Anne Marie Lachaussee, the new owner of the Broken Bone, made the decision to hire him based on his size. This was when things with his life began to turn around and he began to get his affairs in order. I could see how he had been through so much and yet seemed to still hold a positive outlook on his life I could also see that maybe I and Darren had a lot more in common than I thought. I was also developing feelings for Darren that went well beyond that of two friends or even coworkers. I was beginning to develop feelings of love towards Darren. I also knew all about the deep dark secrets that Anne Marie Lachaussee held. The thing was that she had no idea when she hired me that I knew so much about her. I also took quiet comfort in the fact that she knew nothing about who I was. I had a feeling that soon enough she would learn all about who I was and that I knew all of her secrets. I had no idea why she was in Vegas, but I was sure as hell determined to find out and ruin her for what she done to my sister and how those events changed my life as well. I thought, "Anne Marie Lachaussee, you will pay before I am done with you."

9 VAMPIRE STRIPPERS FROM HELL PART 3

Encounter

I have to admit: the whole vampire thing actually works to my advantage at times. I have discovered that working at a strip club I have become accustomed to drinking liquor. Because I am a vampire, alcohol has no effect on me. I am able to drink all I want without any issues. This can be a blessing as well as a curse. I have to watch how much I drink so that I don't draw any suspicions.

It has been three weeks and Anne-Marie Lachaussee still has no clue about who I am. I am still having trouble in determining the exact reason she has made her new home in Las Vegas. I can tell that it has some sinister meaning behind it. I know what this bitch is capable of, especially after seeing what happened to my sister all those years ago. Even though I was not really all that mad about the events that led to me being made, I am angry with Anne-Marie Lachaussee for taking my sister's innocence for her own selfish reasons.

I will deal with that in due time. I have other issues that need to be addressed at the moment. Following the night between Darren and me, he has been in my thoughts and dreams. I have not been able to get him out of my mind regardless of how hard I try. I am torn as to whether to tell Darren the truth or not. I could just imagine that conversation:

"Hi Darren! I think you are a great guy. You're sweet, handsome, well hung, and all in all one hell of a piece of manpower, but I have a secret to tell you. I am a vampire and I have to have sex in an effort to stay alive. So if you don't mind, you will have a vampire fucking you."

Yeah, that would not be awkward at all.

I had to get ready for work; I had no time to concentrate on the issue in front of me at the moment. I had to get to the club and get ready for another fun-filled Saturday night at the Broken Bone. Darren had some errands to run and left a note for me that he would catch up with me at the club. I hopped into my red Camaro and headed into work. I got to the club earlier than usual in an effort to try and catch up with Darren. I wanted to talk to him. I walked in and made my way to the dressing room. I asked one of the girls, Amanda, if Darren had made it in yet.

"No sweetie, he hasn't made it in yet. How are you doing tonight? Looking forward to another busy night of drunken men trying to paw at us like pieces of raw meat?"

"Shit, I am to the point that I'm about to start to cut them off if I get poked one more time by one of these perverts trying to shove their sad excuse for a cock into my pussy. I swear someone is going to become a eunuch."

"Ouch, it's not that bad, is it?"

"It really isn't. I just have a lot going on with me at the moment and I don't know what to do about it."

"You're in love with Darren, aren't you? Come on. Be real. Everyone sees the way you two look at each other. You, with your unspoken language, and the way he talks about you when you are not around. The poor boy can barely work when you are not here. I can tell you that boy is madly in love with you. You need to tell him you feel the same way. Hell, even if you two don't actually get together, you two should just fuck and get it over with."

"That's the problem. We have fucked. I have to admit he was wonderful in bed, but he remembers nothing about it. I am afraid that if he knows, it will ruin our relationship."

"That would be a little of a problem. All I can tell you, sweet tits, is that you need to follow your heart and let it lead you to the right decision."

"Amanda, you are awesome. What would I do without a friend like you?"

"I don't know but if you don't get your ass out there and shake those tits, you are going to be a broke bitch at the end of the night."

I went to my locker and dropped off my outfits for the evening. I have been working on some new numbers. I hoped that my work was going to reward me nicely in the way of tips. It was a holiday weekend in the middle of summer; I had a good chance to clean up over the course of the night. Hell, if it meant getting more tips, I might even let the perverts finger my wet pussy. I changed into my first outfit for the night: a Wonder Woman-type getup that I bought from a local novelty shop, thinking it would be a great idea. I took the stage and worked my magic. After the new DJ, who seemed nervous at seeing a naked woman, screwed my music up for the third time, he finally got it right and I worked my magic. I made $30 in tips on the first song of the night and an additional $20 on the encore song. I made $50 dollars off the bat; my house fee for the night was already paid for, with plenty to spare already.

"Amanda, can you give me a hand? I have a clasp that is stuck."

Amanda was great at helping me in a lot of different ways. If I were a lesbian, I would have jumped at the chance of being with her. She was perfect in a number of ways—long blonde hair, perky round tits, and the most piercing blue eyes that I have ever seen. She has a pussy that is well shaved and always kept up with the utmost of care. Amanda came over to assist me with my wardrobe issues, and as she did, she brushed her hands across my breast. At first, I wanted to pull away, but at the same time, I was turned on a little by the experience. The feel of her hands going across my nipples sent energy through my body.

"I am so sorry, Angela. I didn't mean...."

"It's okay, Amanda. No problem. I've got a little bit of time before I am due on the stage again. I'm going to grab a shower." I walked to the shower area and turned the water on. The feel of the warm water hitting my breast was as relaxing as getting a turn-on. I began to think about what had just happened between Amanda and me, and I began to play with my clit to get a little pleasure at the thought of that goddess who had just brushed her hands across my nipple and made them in an instant stand at attention, begging for more. I began to twist the stud that I had in my left nipple and enjoy the energy shooting through my pussy. While I was busy fingering my wet hole and lost in thought about Amanda, I felt a hand taking one of my nipple rings and giving a moderate tug on it. The sensation brought me from my fantasy. Standing there in the shower with me was Amanda. The sight of her naked body was causing me to get even wetter than I already was. I could almost not contain my excitement at the thought of her giving my body some much-needed attention. Amanda leaned down and took my right nipple into her mouth to begin sucking on it while still teasing my left nipple. I almost had an orgasm just from her sucking on my nipples.

"Yeah baby, suck my tits. I love it when your tongue rubs across my nipple. Please don't stop. I have wanted this from you for so long, but didn't know how to tell you. I have wanted to have sex with you for the longest time. I wish I could easily express my feelings for Darren as I did with you."

"Sweetie, can I be honest with you? I masturbate at work every time I see you on stage. Angela, I am unable to control my feelings. I have wanted to smell your sweet pussy and take in your juices for the longest time. Let me eat your pussy out and show you the true beauty of having a woman tongue fuck your cunt and drive you to a new level of madness."

"Oh god, Amanda, eat my pussy and make me cum. Barely stand up. I want you to take and soak up what my entire wet cunt has to offer. Please fuck me mad with your tongue."

Amanda went to town on my pussy, eating it as if it were a rare food. I enjoyed the sensation of her tongue buried deep into my cunt. It was as if she were looking for new areas that she could manipulate in an effort to drive me as close as she could to climax without allowing it to happen. She had enough experience with other women that she could read their language and tell when they were about to lose all control of their bodies. She would get me to that point and then pull away in an effort to make sure that I was not going to cum until she was ready for me to.

"I want to cum, Amanda. Please let me cum. My body feels like it will explode. I love you eating my snatch, but I really want to cum and let you soak all of me in."

"I will let you cum when the time is right for me and you to release our emotions as well as for us to release our loads in unison."

While I wanted to argue with her, I also had to admit that the feel of her tongue on my pussy lips sent me to a new level of pleasure and every time she tugged on my nipples, I had bolts of energy shoot through me.

"Angela, why don't you meet me in the dressing area? We can continue this in a lot better manner."

"Give me a second to dry off."

"No baby. Come as you are. You will be more than wet when I am finished with you."

A couple of minutes later, I made my way to where Amanda was. She was on her knees with her mouth eagerly waiting for my pussy's arrival. She went back to where she had left off and picked up on the licking almost as if she had not missed a beat. Amanda took a cigarette lighter out of her purse and lit it. I was a little taken aback.

"What are you going to do with that?"

"Giving you the time of your life, trust me."

Taking the flame, she barely placed it against the metal of my nipple ring. Within a few seconds, the metal began to heat up and the sensation sent waves of pleasure through my body. Then she did the same thing with the other nipple. That was all I needed to finish me off. I exploded in a gush of cum that came deep within my pussy; Amanda went down like a kid with a water hose. The sight of her licking up all of my juices made me cum for the second time, giving her more of a gift than she thought.

I was now turned on by the thought of tasting her pussy. I had heard her girlfriend talk about how sweet her snatch was, and I was moments from being able to taste it for myself. The excitement of Amanda and me putting on an impromptu show at the back for the rest of the girls and a few bouncers that were passing through caused me to completely forget my issues with Darren. I got between Amada's soft thighs and took a few licks on her clit. She was already wet.

Her scent was intoxicating. Having her cunt in my face was almost an honor. I was being rewarded for all of my secret dreams: when I was alone in my room finger fucking myself, I thought of eating her pussy out and now I was living out my fantasy in full. I began to finger fuck myself as Amanda began to grind her snatch into my face; I was being smothered with Amanda's cunt, as I eagerly licked all of her juices. She began to gush from the excitement. I looked up long enough to see Amanda with the lighter right at her nipples, the flame from the lighter licking at her nipples and moans of ecstasy being expressed every time the flame hit her nipple. The mere thought of this got both of us to cum at the same time. I wanted to be bathed in her pussy juices and lick every drop of them as quickly as I could. After this, I needed another shower, but I thought, "What the fuck. It'll give the perverts something to fantasize about knowing that two girls went down on each other's pussies."

"Fuck, I am on stage in the next three songs."

I had about enough time to grab a quick cigarette and get changed into my next outfit. The rest of the night went part without too many incidents. Darren and I got the chance to talk when we could. He took care of a few rowdy customers who decided that "no" was not intended for them. All in all, I made about $600 for the night.

I was in the back getting ready to leave when I heard Anne-Marie screaming about some type of issue that she was imagining about this week. I had no idea who she was screaming at, but I would not want to be in their shoes. I finished getting my stuff packed and walked out to my car and left for the night. About halfway home, I realized that I left something back at the club. I made the trip back and headed to the dressing area to grab my make-up case. I heard sounds coming from Anne-Marie's office and the sounds of what seemed like a guy in her office. I walked by the office and saw the door was opened just a crack.

"Oh yeah, baby, lick that clit. You like licking momma's clit, don't you?"

"Oh yeah, Anne-Marie, your pussy is the best I have had in a long time. It is so tight and wet. I could eat your snatch out all day and night and never get tired of it."

That voice sounded familiar. I could have sworn that it sounded like Darren. I pushed the door open just a touch to see, Anne-Marie sitting on the edge of the desk, legs spread. Sure enough, Darren was down in between her legs eating her pussy. Anne-Marie caught a glimpse of me watching and made sure to give me a wink.

"Darren, you fuck me as good as I hear you can, and that head of security position is as good as yours and then you can afford to move out of that skank Angela's shit hole. Hell, if you service me good enough, I might consider letting you stay with me so you can fuck me anytime you want."

Anne-Marie locked eyes on me and made me stand there and watch as the man I cared for deeply fucked her in front of me.

"I want you to slide that large cock inside of me as deep as you can. Don't worry about hurting me. I like it rough."

Anne-Marie cleared her desk off and had Darren mount her. He had no idea I was standing there. I was forced to see him pounding her pussy like a thoroughbred horse.

"There you go, stud. Fuck me real good. I want to feel every thrust of your cock deep into me. I need your large cock to pound me and fuck me like a cheap whore. I bet you would love to be doing this to that whore, Angela, wouldn't you. I bet she would be dying to know that you're fucking her boss to better your job status."

"Angela is nothing to me. She will not give me what I want, but you; you let me fuck you hard. I wish she had let me do this and stop being a pretentious slut who will let any guy fuck her, but won't let me even get close to her."

"You deserve better, and I am more than able to give that to you. You can fuck me anytime that you want. I have no restrictions on when or where you can fuck me. I even like doing it in public. Imagine me waking you up every morning, riding you cowgirl style while you play with my nipples and going to bed pounding my tight little ass while I finger fuck my pussy. You like the taste of me, don't you?"

"Yes Anne-Marie, I'm fixing to cum. Oh God, I'm cumming."

"Yes, sweet Darren, deposit your seed deep inside of me. I want to feel your cum inside my pussy as it fills me up. Oh god, baby cum in me. Make me your cum dump. I want your seed in me to continue my legacy; you are the man I have chosen to impregnate me and allow me to continue my destiny."

I could tell the moment that Darren had dropped a load of cum into Anne-Marie. It was the same face that I saw the night he and I had sex. The spell that she had me under was suddenly released; I knew immediately that she had detected that I was a vampire and that she was placing me under a spell to watch her fuck Darren. He then left the office followed by Anne-Marie.

"Angela, so good to see you're still here. Come into my office. I would like to talk to you. Darren was just leaving; I hope you will think long and hard about my offer, sweet Darren."

"I will. Anne-Marie, see you Friday night."

I went into Anne-Marie's office and she shut the door behind me.

"Sit your little vampire stripper ass

down, you little slut. I saw the performance you and Amanda put on. How do you think your little dream boy would like to know that the woman he has emotions for is a carpet muncher? I know it must have killed you to see him fucking me and knowing that his sperm is inside me, working to knock me up. When I get pregnant, I will have an offspring to carry on my legacy should anything ever happen to me. Listen here, you little bitch, you will do as I say. If you don't, I will tell Darren the truth about you. I will tell him that you are a vampire. And I will show him the video of you getting after Amanda's pussy in the dressing room. If you push me too far, I will make him myself and take him away from you. I haven't made someone since that student years ago."

"You fucking bitch! That was my sister that you made. That led her to make me one night and here I am. So you want to play games. Remember I can get to him before you do. I would hate it if my fangs retract and I accidentally bite him."

"Enough! You will do as I say or I will fucking ruin your life before you can say blood. You will go home and in the morning kick him out of your apartment; you will never talk to him here at work and he will not come to your rescue any more. I took your precious little sister and I will take your boyfriend or kill him in the process. Besides I have someone who I have hired to begin working here as one of the new girls. You might know her. Her name is Tracy Ann Madison; she will be the new piece of pussy that your precious Darren will be interested in. In fact, you are going to stay here while your sister goes to your apartment to crash for the night. She will seduce him and glamour him into wanting her. By the time you get home, he will have forgotten about your tired old snatch, as he will have Tracy here who has a perpetual hymen. Let's face it: guys love a pussy that is always tight and ready to grip their cocks."

"Sorry, sis. You are yesterday's news. There is a new bitch in town and her name is Tracy Ann Madison. I will make sure to record Darren fucking me and leave a copy in your room. That way you will feel like you are there. I think I will even fuck him on your sheets in your bed. You make any attempts to stop me and my mistress, and we will bury you. I have a new life and have learned new powers, while your tired ass is still stuck in the 1800s. You have lost and we, the stronger, have won in the battle of good and evil. You can either join us or be destroyed."

"I knew it. Why are you so determined to sink your teeth into Darren? Why not just leave me and him alone and allow us to be happy?"

"Because to do so would allow you to have a happy life, the storybook ending that was destined to be for me, you bitch," Tracy Ann said.

Anne-Marie and Tracy locked me in the office and tied me to a chair; I was trapped, knowing that the man I loved was about to be made a victim of my slut sister and that vixen of a mistress, Anne-Marie Lachaussee. I needed a way out of this situation, or I was going to lose the one man that I honestly knew I loved and my sister would have taken just one more thing from me and I would have nothing left to lose in my life.

10 VAMPIRE STRIPPERS FROM HELL PART 4

Boiling Point

My decision to work at the Broken Bone was based on what a couple of the girls I ran into had to say about the management. I was told the management understood if one of the girls had to take a night off. This was all before the new owner showed up and took complete control of things. This former management was nowhere to be seen and many wondered where they had gone. They never even showed up for their last checks.

I had a pretty good idea where they were. I was afraid that they would not be coming back. I knew the type of person that Anne-Marie Lachaussee was. I knew that she would not rest until she got what it was that she was after. I knew that the sooner that I was able to get out of this office, the sooner I would be able to save Darren.

I knew the situation. I knew I could lose Darren after Tracy glamoured him—or worse she would make him. If he fought too much, she would kill him by draining all of his blood. I had to get out and do it soon. I was about to give up when the office door opened up and Mark, one of the bouncers, came through the door at a hurried pace.

"Angela, what is going on? Are you all right?"

"No time to explain, Mark. I need you to come with me. I have a bad feeling about something." I came out of the door and was greeted by Amanda.

"Girl, what the fuck is going on?"

"I can't explain. You and Mark, come with me. I need to get to my house in a hurry. I feel bad things are about to happen."

The three of us got into my Camaro and sped towards my apartment.

"This is a matter of life and death. Anne-Marie has gone off the deep end and is looking to do bad things to Darren to get at me. I need to get to him before she does."

The trip to my apartment seemed to take forever. I had a million things going through my mind about what could happen if they reached the apartment before me. I was hoping that Darren had decided to stop off for a few drinks before heading home. That would give me the time I needed to stop these two evil bitches before they ruined my life.

We reached my apartment and I was in luck. Darren was not home. I still had a chance to stop things. I walked into my apartment and saw Tracy and Anne-Marie standing there.

"Well, well, looks like we are going to have a little party. Angela, you brought spectators to watch as we take turns fucking the life out of Darren. So Amanda, has Angela here told you her little secret as to how she and I are so close?"

"Don't fucking do it, Anne-Marie. This has nothing to do with her or Mark; this is between me, you, and my sister."

"I beg to differ; I feel that Amanda needs to know who it was that was eating her pussy like a prisoner on a three-day release. I think that Amanda needs to know that you are not who you say you are. She needs to know that you are a vampire and that you are over 140 years old. Maybe that is the truth that she needs to know."

"What the fuck, I had sex with a vampire? I showered with you on a regular basis. Were you just waiting for the right time before you finally bit my neck and turned me into the same type of freak that you are? Damn bitch, where the hell is the holy water when I need it? I will straight up send your ass back to hell or wherever your blood-sucking ass came from."

Amanda was angry. I couldn't let this go.

"Hey, Anne-Marie, why don't you tell her that you're a vampire and that you are the reason that I am the way that I am?"

"Tell her how you made my sister and how Tracy made me later. I bet you are not too eager to reveal that. Why not tell her that you came here to make Darren? Tell her how you fucked him back at the club and encouraged him to cum inside you to get you pregnant. Tell her about your plan to turn all of the dancers at the club into vampires and how you want to turn all of Las Vegas into one large breeding ground for vampires. While you had me locked in your office, I was able to read the notes on your desk. I know all about your plan and I am here to stop it."

"Now Amanda, you can hate me, you can condemn me if you want, but I would ask you to wait to do that after you have taken out this bitch and saved your own ass. She's the one you need to fear."

To this day, I still remember how I was made by my sister. I have no idea why she became obsessed with making me. I was no threat to her, but she felt that she had to make me in an effort to save herself. I remember the events that led to her making me and transforming me forever.

"I would like to tell you, Amanda, what she did to me. Why don't you pull up a chair and I will tell you all about this bitch I used to call a sister."

I was out one night years after Tracy disappeared; my family and I assumed she was dead. We were not sure what happened. I needed to clear my head and deal with some stuff that was going on in my life. I went to one of the local watering holes to drown my sorrows. A few hours later, I felt a hand grab me by the shoulder.

"Angela, is that you?" The voice sounded familiar but I didn't think it could be my long-lost and feared dead sister.

Angela stopped and took a breath.

"Tracy, is that really you? Where the hell have you been all these years? We thought you were dead," she went on.

"I might as well be. The story is a long one. You should come with me." Tracy led me to one of the back rooms, and closed and locked the door behind us.

Angela stopped again, as if telling the story was draining her energy. She started again.

"What is going on? Why are you locking me in? And where have you been?"

Then my sister said, "Trust me. This is for the best, sister. As far as the family is concerned, I am dead; as far as you are concerned, well, that is a little more complicated. Come back with me to my place. I will be able to explain everything there."

We proceeded back to her place where she had a nice little setup for herself. I had to admit it was a little dark for my taste but it was not too bad. Tracy turned me around and looked deep into my eyes. "Angela, forgive me, sister, for what I am about to do, but I need to do it for both of our sakes. You will find me very attractive and will do as I tell you. Trust me. This is for your own good."

Tracy-Ann reached up and slowly began to unbutton my blouse; I have had enough experience to know which way this was going to go. The last button was free, and then Tracy-Ann threw open my blouse. I arched my back, allowing it to fall off my arms while at the same time presenting my tits for her inspection. She reached between my large mounds and undid the hook that held my massive melon's hostage in their fabric prison.

Tracy-Ann's eyes lit up upon seeing my creamy tits eager to be licked. Tracy-Ann leaned down and began to suck on one of my nipples; the feel of her tongue on my nipple sent bolts of electrical current pulsing through my body, and I could feel the juices of my pussy beginning to open the floodgates and gushes of hot juice shooting from my cunt. Tracy-Ann noticed the smell that my cunt was giving off; she undid my jeans where a mild wet spot was beginning to form from the dripping pussy that was encased in my panties.

Tracy-Ann slid two fingers down to the front of my panties and began to tease my clit. It quivered at the thought that in a matter of seconds to minutes, she was going to fuck me with her tongue. Feeling her sliding her fingers into my hole made be so glad that I was bisexual. Having a man play with my pussy and eat my snatch out was great, but sometimes only a woman can give you the feeling that you really need, as she knows how to play your clit like a violin. Tracy-Ann whispered into my ear, "I want to eat that hot wet cunt of yours. I want you to cum in my face and I want to drink your juices."

Tracy-Ann slid down and removed my panties with her teeth. I slipped out of my jeans and boots, and we both made out way to the bed. I grabbed the bottom of Tracy-Ann's T-shirt and lifted it up over her head. To my surprise, she was going without a bra and I knew that she was seeking a woman out to have a sexual fling with and I happened to be the right person for the job. Her tits were as close to perfect as you could get. I inhaled one of her tits into my mouth. The feel of a woman's bare breast in my mouth was a very cathartic experience for me. I reached down while sucking on her tits and began to play with her pussy; her juices were pouring out of her by the gallon, and I got between her thighs and began to take in all of her juices. The feeling was nothing I had ever had before; I wanted her to just pour out into my mouth.

"Why don't we do 69?" Tracy-Ann suggested. At this point, I was good with anything she suggested as long as my and her pussies and mouths were all involved in the equation. Her tongue darting in and out of my pussy was amazing; she was a pro at fucking a woman with her mouth. I felt her teeth bite down gently on my clit and give it a tug; this sent another torrent of juices down into her face where she lapped it up like a person in the desert with water. The feel of her mouth sucking on my clit was amazing. I was quickly becoming into a woman possessed with getting my pussy eaten.

After I drained what seemed like a gallon or more from my pussy, Tracy-Ann rolled me over and said, "Get up on your knees."

This was an odd request I thought, but I will try anything once. I got up on all fours when I felt a tongue shoot rapidly into my asshole; this was new for me and I was taken aback by it. This was obviously something that she was used to doing, and I looked between my legs and saw Tracy-Ann feverishly working her snatch over with a couple of fingers. The sight of a woman frigging herself while eating another woman's ass out was actually hot to watch. The thought actually got me to gushing again. Finally, Tracy-Ann let out a moan that was part pleasure and part wild animal. After the wild sex I had just had, I needed a nap. Tracy-Ann put me back together and took my drenched panties so she could remember the time we had.

Then I realized that this was a dream and was trying to wake up when I felt the sharp pain of two fangs digging into my neck. I suddenly woke up to see Tracy perched over me with blood dripping from her fangs. They quickly retracted back into her mouth and then she took off. A few hours later, I woke up again and realized three things: firstly, I needed a shower, secondly, I had not eaten yet, and thirdly, I was extremely tired from Tracy feeding off me. I decided to order room service and then take a shower while I was waiting.

In the shower, I could still smell Tracy on me as I thought about the wild sex we had just had a few hours earlier. The thought made me horny again; I told myself I was not going to play with my pussy again. Instead, I took the time to play with my nipples; my soaped-up breasts got me turned on. I enjoyed looking at myself naked. I took the chance to explore all of my body and wondered what it meant that I enjoyed having sex so much. Was I a nymphomaniac?

If I were, I could live with this and be good with the fact. Whatever the reason, I was determined to not stop having sex until I was either dead or my pussy fell off either through rough sex, old age, over-usage, or a weird combination of all of the above. Nonetheless, I enjoyed sex and I could easily get a partner from either sex to provide me with a thrill on a regular basis.

"Amanda, that is the story of how this skank here made me into what I am. Unlike her and her vampire whore of a maker, I only feed on humans when I need to and I usually prefer humans that are freshly dead or ones who will not be missed in society. I am in no way a threat to you. These two on the other hand are up to no good, and if you are not careful, they will dine off your blonde ass. If you have never trusted me before, I am asking you to do so now."

Anne-Marie made a lunge for Amanda and I could tell what she was going for. I had only one thing left to do, and that was to show my dedication to Amanda. I took the picture frame off the table and threw it up in the direction of Anne-Marie; the immediate sight of her reflection was more than enough to stop her progress. As any vampire would know, the sight of his or her reflection would drive a vampire crazy and cause him or her to become weak in an instant. Tracy ran for her mistress, and I knew that I had to do the same to her or she would finish what Anne-Marie had started. Again, I threw the mirror in her direction and watched her fall to the floor beside her mistress.

"I should kill both of you, but I feel generous tonight. Do not mistake my kindness for weakness. You look at Darren as much and I will finish what I started here tonight. I may not be as old as you bitches, but I am smart when it comes to dealing with dried-up rags like you two. Mike, remove these pieces of garbage from my apartment."

Mike took both of them and tossed them out of the apartment, but not before getting a good old feel of some vampire tits.

Amanda looked at me.

"Whoa, what the fuck was that shit? A few hours ago, you were eating my pussy like a seafood buffet and now, I almost became the buffet for a couple of crazy ass vampire bitches and found out that my best friend is a vampire. I just need to get home and take all of this in. I will say thank you for saving my ass."

"You're welcome. I hope that this does not change things too much between us. I really wanted to tell you, but I had no way to do so. I hope that we can still be friends, but I understand if you feel you cannot trust me."

I had just changed into my robe after taking a shower to relax from all of the crazy things that had been going on since I saw Darren fucking Anne-Marie. A couple of minutes later, there was a knock at the door. I went and opened it to see Darren, who had obviously left his house keys at home when he left earlier that day.

"Angela, we need to talk. I need to talk to Anne-Marie. The last I saw of her was at the club when we were in a... um meeting. She said that she had an offer for me, and I wanted to talk to her about it. I went by her house but she was not there; her cell keeps going to voice mail. I really need to talk to her."

"Darren, I talked to her after you left and she said that she had some business to take care out of town and she would be back in a few days. I am sure you can talk about the offer when she gets back. I would not worry about it. Why not just relax? I will make some dinner and we can just try to relax and put this evening behind us."

I caught him sneaking a peak down my robe. I had mixed feelings: the first was I was upset that he was peeking; the other part was turned on that he was staring at my breasts in my robe. I thought fast and made the decision to play the game and see what would happen. I managed to loosen the tie of my robe without him noticing. I rose up from drying my hair and sure enough, the robe fell open. Here I was in all my naked glory. What would he do? Turn away and leave, or make a move? It was obvious what was going through his mind. He was thinking his reaction over; it took about three seconds to see his reaction. He made his move; he walked over and tried to act as if he was trying to assist me.

His hand went inside my robe and found its way on my breast. My clit blazed furiously, making warm, slick pussy juice seep to my cunt lips, preparing me for Darren's advances. I had no idea where this was going to lead me, but I was more than ready for anything that was to come from the encounter. I turned him around and saw the massive fuck stick that was sticking out in a tent from his pants. I reached down and undid his belt, allowing me to unbutton his pants. It was then that I saw, sticking out of his boxers, his enormous thirteen-inch-long prick.

I was amazed at the large size of his member. I had to admit it was one of the larger ones I had seen in quite a while. The mere thought of this being inside of me again made me all wet and horny. He made a quick work of the rest of his clothes and soon was standing in front of me naked and ready. I was eager to go down and begin working on his balls, taking in all of his essence as much as I could. The smell of his manhood was intoxicating and led my nipples to harden once again. After taking care to give his large egg-shaped balls a thorough tongue bath, I proceeded to work over his large fuck rod.

"Fuck me, you big stud. Show me the power of your prick and make me your whore for the night."

These words seemed to just fly from my lips without any real efforts at all.

He picked me up and bent me over the counter. He removed my robe from my wet naked body in the process. He placed a little spit on the end of his knob and on the opening of my asshole, and then with a massive thrust, I felt his entire member shoot inside of me all the way to the balls.

The feel of his balls against the opening of my pussy sent me over the edge. "Fuck me hard, and give it to me. Fuck my brains out and make me beg for your cock, you hell of a man."

The more I screamed out for him to fuck me, the harder he responded and pounded me. He reached around, grabbed a hold of my tits, and used them to get more of a bit of advantage in his wild fucking of my asshole.

My clit was on fire and I was not going to be satisfied until he fucked my throbbing cunt; three encounters today and this was the first one in which I was going to get a real professional who knew how to fuck a woman's pussy.

Again I was possessed with the spirit of a sex-starved whore, as I blurted out, "Eat me!" I pleaded, "Eat my pussy. I need your tongue inside of me to make me feel complete. My clit is on fire and it needs your tongue to extinguish the flames." I spread my legs and parted my lips for him to make a direct entrance into my snatch. He dove in and stopped short of entering me with his tongue; instead, he began playing with my clit. The sensation caused me to arch my back, placing my dripping wet cunt further into his face. The feel of his face between my legs taking in my wet cunt sent energy through my body.

"I'm on the verge of cumming.... Oh

fucking GOD! My fucking pussy is going to fucking cummmmm!"

At that moment, I could not take it anymore. I exploded and sent a massive gush of my juices right into his face. The look of my pussy juice dripping from his face was a clear sign to him and me that he had done a remarkable job.

I was still on fire and was not satisfied with this encounter ending like this. I wanted him inside me again and I was willing to do anything I had to in an effort to get his cock into me. As if he were reading my mind, he took the prick that had torn through my asshole and began to slide it deep inside my wet hole. The feel of his entire thirteen inches filling me up made me more eager for him to pound my cunt.

"Forget the love-making shit; fuck me like a cheap slut. I want and need to be fucked. I want you to pound me to the point that people three rooms down will know that I am getting my brains fucked out by you. Fuck me! Fuck me! Fuck me!" I kept screaming in hopes of getting him to pound my pussy with a passion that I had not had in quite some time. I looked up at him and told him to drive his hard prick between my tits. I wanted him to tit fuck me like there was no tomorrow.

"I want you to tit fuck me while I finger fuck my wet pussy."

As he slid his cock into the crevice between my tits, I drove two fingers into my wet snatch. The motion of him going up and down and riding my tits made me wetter than I already was. The feel of this made me want to get off by finger fucking my pussy that much more. After a half hour of wild sex, I was fucking my cunt with such passion that I could feel my palm hitting my clit and sending waves of passion through me. Finally, without notice, the volcano that had been Darren erupted on me; jets of hot ooze came from his hard prick splashing on my tits as well as my face. I had seen a lot of cum, but this had to be the richest cum I had ever seen. I thought to myself, "Good thing he did not cum inside of me. I would have been pregnant for sure."

I had to make my move. I knew the only way to save Darren from Tracy, and Anne-Marie, was to do the one thing I had tried to avoid doing the entire time and that was making Darren into a vampire. I knew the old methodology that if mortals had been bit by a vampire, they would be the eternal slave of the person that bit them. I knew that Anne-Marie had made a fatal mistake in not biting Darren and that the only way he could become hers was if he was bit. The act of fucking was not enough to make a person; she would have to bite his cock while going down on him just as she bit Tracy's pussy lips when she made her.

That cunt may have taken my sister, but she would never have the man I loved. What I did next took me by surprise as it did Darren. I bent over him, sank my fangs into his neck, and began to feed off of him; at first, he had fear in his eyes, and then he relaxed and the bite was more of pleasure than it was of pain. I fed until I knew that I had done what was necessary to make Darren mine. Tracy and Anne-Marie would sense this, and if they, for whatever reason, did not, then biting and feeding his blood would be poison to them and they would become weak and unable to defend them against an attack.

"You... you are a vampire, and you just bit me. Why would you do that? I thought you loved me...."

"Darren, I have no time to explain now. You need to rest. I will explain all to you when you wake up. For now, you need your energy and need to rest. Just know I had reasons for why I did what I did and you will hopefully understand very soon."

11 VAMPIRE STRIPPERS FROM HELL PART 5

Sexual Hunger

The next morning, I got up and made breakfast for Darren and me. I knew that there were a lot of questions that he was going to have, and I prayed all night that I had made the right choice.

I would not be able to live with myself in knowing that I had made a mortal into a vampire and after all of that, Darren left me anyway. I did not want to sacrifice him for nothing. I needed to take a little time and get the right mood set for the talk that I was hoping to have with him. I heard him getting out of bed and held my breath, hoping he would not come out of his room and immediately confront me about what had happened the night before.

"Morning Angela, I see you made

breakfast. Smells good."

"Look, about last night, we need to talk."

"What's to talk about? We fucked. You returned the favor by biting my neck and turning me into a vampire. I see nothing to talk about. As I see it, things are pretty much cut and dried. By the way, thanks for making me into a vampire. I was living such a boring life, and I guess fucking Anne-Marie for job security was too much for you to handle. Boy, this will be tough to explain to Anne-Marie."

"That's what I wanted to talk to you about. I know what happened between you and Anne-Marie last night; I know that you fucked her in exchange for the promotion to head of security. The truth of the matter is that she had a motive behind her actions. Anne-Marie is a vampire; she wanted you to cum inside of her to get her pregnant. She then came here to have my sister seduce you and bite you. This would have made you her slave."

"I know I bit you and made you my slave and that was wrong, but I had my reasons. I have wanted you ever since I first met you. I wanted to tell you that I am a vampire and that I love you, but I never had the courage to tell you. Last night, what happened was not the first time that you fucked me. You actually fucked me the night that we got drunk.

The reason that you do not remember has nothing to do with the alcohol. I glamoured you. This means that I controlled your thoughts to make you forget that we had sex. I know that was wrong, but I did not want that to ruin our relationship. But I see that I might have done that any way without even trying."

"Let me get this straight: you made me a vampire to keep me for yourself all because you love me, and I am to believe that Anne-Marie is also a vampire and was plotting to steal me away from you just for her selfish reasons. I honestly was hoping that you would have a better explanation than this. I mean really, so what do we do now when you and I are not able to go out into the sun for long periods of time? I really do not want to discuss this any further."

Amanda came by a few minutes later to talk to me about last night.

"Hey Angela, I want to apologize for my overreaction; the whole thing with you, Anne-Marie, your sister, and them being obsessed with biting Darren to steal him was just a little much to digest. Did Darren ever come home last night?"

"Hi Amanda, I'm right here, and yes, I have a hickey from hell thanks to Angela here. So you are telling me that she was telling the truth about what happened?

That I was the target of some freakish vampire that was aiming to control me for her personal sex slave?"

"Pretty much, that seems to be the way things seemed to be going, and had it not been for my girl here, I would have been the main course for a couple of hungry vampire bitches. Hey sweet tits, I got to head to the club and see if there is anything left of my stuff. I have a feeling that I am going to encounter a couple of angry vampires after last night, so I am taking my mirror with me. I saw the result it had last night, so hopefully it will work again if I need it to."

"Okay sweetie, take care. I will be there later to turn in my resignation. I have a couple of friends that have some connections and might be able to get me on there. You should come with me, and we can be a hell of a duo."

"Shit, I have no idea what I am going to do. I think that the stripping game is just getting too complicated for me. I just want to get my stuff from my locker and get home and forget the last 24 hours even happened. I will come by later."

Darren and I sat back down to finish breakfast; the rest of the morning was uneventful as we sat there and talked more about things in our life, and I found out that he had just recently went through a divorce. In fact, it was only finalized a week ago.

"Wait, that means that the night that we fucked, you were still technically married."

"Yep, I was still legally married to the woman that I thought was going to be my everything for the rest of my life. Instead, she turned out to be less than I had thought."

"I am so sorry. I had no idea that you were married."

"Let me buy you dinner tonight. It has been awhile since I got to spend the night with a gorgeous woman. It's been ever since my wife left me."

"What happened if I may ask?"

"Apparently, she could not handle my large penis. That and the fact that I tend to fuck rather hard; this was just too much for her to take, and she just left me."

"What a bitch," I could not believe that I had just said that without even thinking. "I am so sorry, I did not mean...."

"It's okay. She was a bitch; she took everything from the house that was not nailed down and tried to destroy everything of mine. Apparently, she had an awakening when she realized that my enormous cock being shoved into her pussy was morally wrong. Explain that shit: a husband fucking his wife is looked at being morally wrong."

Later on, Darren and I went to one of the local bars and took a little time to just sit and talk. I had made sure to wear one of my favorite sweaters as well as my revealing undergarments, in case things progressed to that point again. We enjoyed each other's company. He had shown a lot of progress in regard to opening up a lot to talk to me and tell me what was going on in his life. We lost track of time and before long, we both realized that we had to leave. Darren and I walked to my apartment.

"I must admit, Angela, that I really enjoyed tonight. It was nice being able to sit and talk to a woman and not having to worry about what it was that she was thinking about me sitting here and spilling my entire life story out to her. I wish tonight did not have to end. Even with this new issue that has come up, I feel a strong connection between us and I feel that we should see where this takes us."

"Who says it has to end right now? After all, I have nothing to do tonight. You have the day off tomorrow, if you even still want to work with that crazy bitch Anne-Marie. Why can't two adults enjoy the company of one another and just be who they are?"

Darren came across the room and

placed a hand on my shoulder, "Angela, I have never wanted a woman as bad as you since my wife left. If I am not being too forward, I want to fuck you again and feel what a real woman can offer without all of the drama that is attached."

At the sound of this, I could feel my nipples harden in anticipation of the upcoming fuck session. I had weird feelings going through me. Deep down, this was not about sex but instead about being with a man and feeling him take command of me in a way I have never felt.

Darren walked back across the room with a look on his face as if he had just made a large mistake in letting his feelings be known. I saw this look and knew I had to do something for both of our sakes. Darren needed a real woman to have sex with, and I needed to have him to fuck me silly. I removed my top and tossed it on the chair. Unhooking the hooks on the front of my bra, my tits became free and took a natural fall from the bra. Slipping out of my jeans, I called to Darren.

"Darren, I need you inside of me. I need you to fuck me like a cheap whore. I need a large cock inside me, and you need a woman that can appreciate all that you can offer."

Darren turned around to see the sight in front of him, and I could quickly see his eagerness at what I had said. He took in the sight of seeing me standing there with a wet spot forming on my red silk panties. I gave a little shake to get my tits to help in the removal of my bra. As it hit the floor, Darren darted across the room and over to me. His grasping of my tits was like nothing I had ever felt before.

The feel of his fingers digging into my large flesh mounds sent a feeling of wanting him, which shot through my body. I could see the outline of his large cock tenting out from the jeans that he was wearing. Darren yanked the jeans off and quickly was ready to go; the sight of his prong in his tighty-whities was more than I could stand, and I was ready for him to embrace me and let our bodies become one with each other in the throes.

Of passion, I reached down and grabbed his tool as I began to work it over with one hand and finger fuck my pussy with the other. Darren reached up and took my nipples in his fingertips. Giving them a gentle twist, I had electric current shooting through my body and a blast of juice shot from my eagerly awaiting hole.

He guided me towards the bed and placed himself between my legs. Starting to kiss my calves, he slowly made his way up. His lips tickled the inside of my right thigh as his soft hair on the back of his head brushed the inside of my left. His hands moved up my hips to the sides of my panties and slowly pulled them down. As he slid them off my feet, he lowered his head down to my pubic mound. His tongue started to slowly tease the outer lips of my pussy, gently caressing them, darting in and out of my juicy hole. His mouth opened and he started to suck on my mound, his tongue flicking against my clit, soon sending electric shocks through my body.

He continued to eat out my pussy for another 15 minutes, the sensations of his expert ministrations moving through my body in waves. His tongue was smooth and silky as it played with my inner and outer lips. His fingers were gentle as they probed my insides. The feel of his lips inside me was almost like nothing I had experienced ever before.

"Eat my pussy. Come on, eat me. Fuck my hole with your tongue and make me feel like the bad girl I am. Come on. Eat my pussy the way you used to eat her pussy out. She was never good enough for you and did not deserve to have your tongue in her skanky ass. You are a man that has a true talent and I want you to drive that tongue deep into me and play with my clit like a lollipop."

I could not believe the words that were being driven out of me. Like a whore that was in the middle of a wild fuck fest, I lost all control, wanted to have my brains fucked out of me, and was willing to go as long as my fuck partner could.

After about 15 minutes, he stood and dropped his tighty-whities to the floor. His rampant erection was throbbing with his heartbeat. I leaned up and pulled back his foreskin. I started to lick the head of his organ; the shiny silky precum that he had been leaking had a slightly salty taste. I parted my lips and enveloped the top three inches of his cock in my mouth. He placed his hands gently on the sides of my head and started to rock back and forth slowly in and out of my mouth. I could feel the smooth gliding of his foreskin up and down his shaft as his knob glided over my tongue. I pulled away from his cock and again lay back on the bed with my legs spread. This was an open invitation for him to put himself inside of me. My pussy was as ready as it was ever going to be, and I wanted cock in me now.

I scooted back as he lay on top of me and guided his spear into my awaiting tunnel. The fullness that I felt was familiar and welcoming. I love the feel of a man's ridged member penetrating me, as their rods explore my pussy looking for the perfect place to position itself in an effort to drive me into a fuck crazy fit. He started to move in and out. I could feel the lips of my pussy grip the shaft of his cock in an attempt to hold onto it until they had been satisfied with the fullness of his large fuck rod. My pussy was quivering as I felt each stroke become more and deeper with each thrust.

While Darren was playing my pussy like a violin, the head of his organ repeatedly hit my G-spot as he pistoned in and out of my tight wet hole. I lost complete and total control of myself; I began to shout out.

"Fuck me harder. Come on, big man. Give me that hard cock in my wet pussy. You like fucking my wet hole with your big member; I bet you want to cum inside me, don't you?"

With every stroke, I was begging him to fuck me harder and harder. I wanted his thick cock to slam into my hole and make me feel like a $2 whore while he fucked my brains out. It had been a while since I had a man like Darren. I could feel his cock beginning to swell inside of me and heard his breath quicken in pace. I knew that he was close, and I threw myself forward against his chest. I backed my pussy off his cock and slowly slid down to my knees. I started to lick his cock head once more and caressed his shaft with my right hand. The taste of my juices on his shaft had me hotter than I had ever been. I had tasted my juices before, but the taste of them on this man's cock had me wetter than anything. While working over his fuck stick, I continued to work my hole over with two fingers. My golden honey was running down my fingers.

Darren then drove his erupting member as deep as he could inside of me. "Cum in me. Let me have your hot, thick creamy man seed deep inside my pussy." I could feel the first blast enter my pussy. Pulling out quickly, blasts three and four went all over my eagerly awaiting tits. The feel of his hot load on my erect nipples drove me to the point of orgasm, and I let out a huge gush that shot from my pussy.

I then felt a tongue from behind and quickly realized that Darren had taken to licking my ass out. For some reason, this sent chills up my spine and made my snatch quiver. With every lick of my ass, I became more passionate in finger fucking my trimmed furburger. This drove both of us to the point that we could not take it anymore. Darren and I were almost in harmony as we let out a massive orgasm at the same time. I could feel the sheets underneath me become drenched as both of our juices combined to make one giant wet spot.

As we both came to a rest on the bed, I could feel the wet spot that we had created and the feeling of that made me smile from ear to ear. I reached over and grabbed the pack of Marlboros off the nightstand, and lit one. I offered Darren one and he politely declined. The afterglow of having one of the wildest screws in the last couple of days, along with the cigarettes that I was enjoying, made me feel complete. It was my sign that when I wanted a smoke after having sex, my fuck partner had done something right. We spent the rest of the night sitting there and talking about all sorts of things.

Darren had some errands to run the next day; I was not in the mood to go out after what had happened.

"I will see you later, Darren. I hope we can talk some more when you get back. We need to get things between us worked out and see where things lead us."

"I will be back in a little while. Take care."

I decided to go back to bed and relax. It was my first real day away from the club after the events that had transpired, and the day was getting off to a horrible start; I woke up to discover that my heating unit was not working. This meant that the room was a balmy 38 degrees. Normally, when I wake up to my nipples being stiff as a board, it is something that I enjoy;

however, this was a different situation and I was not the least a bit happy. I ordered Chinese food and lit a cigarette while waiting for my meal. I planned to take a shower after eating my breakfast.

The feel of the hot water hitting my ice-cold body was a welcomed relief from the icebox that I awoke to a half hour earlier. While in the shower, I decided to give myself a little self-pleasure. "At least I could get a little enjoyment from this morning that was quickly going to hell in a hand basket."

I took a couple of fingers and began to work my clit in a circular motion; the feel of the warm water was inviting and led to my clit standing up for more attention from me. There was a slight feeling of energy that shot through my body, and then I took the two fingers and began to work the inside of my cunt with gentle motions. This was not like many times when it was a finger fuck fest; this was meant to simply just be a little enjoyment in the shower. The feel of my fingers caused the lips of my pussy to begin to quiver a little bit. Just when things were about to get interesting, the doorbell rang.

In my haste, I ran to the door without a stitch of clothing on. It was the same delivery boy from the other day; at least it was someone who has seen me naked before. While the urge to jump his bones

came over me, I took a $20 bill out of my
wallet and gave it to him for his quick
service. Sitting there eating breakfast, I
worked on with my job search. This was a
tiresome task, and I quickly got tired with
it and decided to finish my playtime with
my clit.

Lying on the bed, I began to play with
my nipples. I enjoy tit torture and love to
have my nipples worked over. I began to
play and feel the tugging of my nipples in
the tips of my fingers. This sent waves of
pleasure down to my cunt that was still
wet from the shower; at the same time, a
little of my pussy juices were beginning to
mix with the water from the shower. While
still working my nipples over, I slid the
other hand down to my wet clit. I began to
play with my pussy and was really getting
into the feel of my fingers as they were
drove into my eagerly awaiting snatch.

After a few minutes of this, I began
working my pussy over with a little more
passion as well as tugging on my nipples
with a lot more aggression. In all of the
excitement in the bedroom, I never heard
the door open and the maintenance man
even come in. I was laying there, groaning
and working my pussy into a frenzy, when
I looked up and saw the repairman
standing there watching the show.

"What the fuck, man? Why the hell are

you standing there watching me frig myself with my fingers? Did you enjoy the show? Were you hoping that it would be you in between my legs working my pussy over?"

"I'm... sorry, ma'am. You have such a beautiful body that I was just taken aback by the sight of your body and you working your snatch over. Please don't be mad. I have never done anything like this in my life and I really need this job."

"Do you like the sight of my naked body laying here with me all exposed, my nice round tits with their nipples standing up begging for attention? My snatch wet with my pussy juice? I bet you would love to come here and lick my pussy to taste my juices, wouldn't you? Be honest. You want to fuck me in the worst way."

"Yes... Yes, ma'am. I do want to fuck you. Please don't tell my boss or my wife. We have been through so much. I will do anything to keep you from telling my wife and boss."

"You said anything, correct? Then I tell you what: I feel generous and am willing to make you an offer. I will take this coin out of my purse, and you will call it. If you are correct, you get to fuck my brains out. If not, then you have to watch as I fuck your wife with you in the same room. Do we have a deal?"

"Yes, ma'am. We have a deal. I call

heads."

As I flipped the coin, I had already decided that regardless of the outcome, this repairman was going to service me one way or the other. "Heads it is, Maytag boy. You get to fuck one hot piece of my pussy. Now why don't you get those pants off and get over here to fulfill your wildest dream."

I didn't have to tell him twice as he took his shirt off and quickly took his pants off to reveal his boxer brief underwear; the large lump in front of his brief made me lick my lips as I wanted to get a hold of that large piece of man meat in my mouth. When he dropped his underwear to reveal the large cock that he had concealed, the sexual desire in my body rose a good two hundred percent and I was ready to swallow that cock. I took the head of it into my mouth and began to nurse on the end of it while working my pussy over.

I could not stand it anymore. I wanted and needed that cock in my mouth and proceeded to swallow the entire 9" without a moment's hesitation. The feel of his large member going down my throat was amazing.

"Ohhh, yeah. Suck that large cock, you fucking whore. Take all of my meat down to your whore ass mouth. You suck cock better than my wife ever did."

The sound of him talking to me like this actually shocked me as well as turned me on and made me want his cock that much more. I was now frigging myself with three fingers while he forcefully fed me his anaconda cock down my throat. It had been a long time since a man took charge of me and made me his fuck toy. I had missed the days of wild sex, the kind that afterwards, there is a trip to the furniture store to replace a piece of furniture. The last time I had such an encounter was back in Dallas while on vacation for a week.

Steve was fulfilling all of my needs. There was only one way that this was going to end, and it was with his cum in all of my three holes. The force in which he was feeding me his tube steak was almost with precision, as if he knew exactly what it was that he was doing. No matter the reason, I was enjoying how he was making me crave his cock in my mouth. I could feel his load beginning to enter the chamber; I knew it was not going to be long before his fuck pistol was shooting a load of cum down my throat. Steve grabbed the back of my head and held it there as he blasted the first load of hot spunk down my throat. I swallowed his load with a sense of glee and did not try to resist. Just when I thought he was finished, another blast hit my tongue and

I swallowed it as if it were a prime rib.

Steve withdrew his cock from my mouth and began to eat my pussy with the same type of aggression that he had given me with his cock. I actually thought at one point that he was going to tear my clit off with his teeth. Nonetheless, I was enjoying the aggressive manner in which Steve was going after my pussy. It was apparent that he was a professional at eating pussy and I had to wonder the way he was eating mine: didn't his wife let her husband eat her muff? I could not imagine a woman who was not willing or even eager for her husband to take his tongue and eat her pussy. It was a feeling like no other and all the women I knew loved to have it done to them.

"Eat that pussy, you mad man. Eat my pussy like you do every night that you are going down on your wife. I bet she loves it when you are in between her legs, fucking her cunt with your tongue. That is an amazing feeling to have. That whore does not deserve you; I want a big ex-con to fuck my pussy and make me cum like I have never cum before."

I felt like a woman that was being possessed simply because I had an ex-con that had spent time in prison fucking my tight hole with his mouth and drinking all of my juices. The more I thought about his time in prison, the more I wanted him to drive that prick deep into my snatch and fuck me like he was on a congeal visit.

"Take that cock of yours and drive it deep into me. Fuck my hole like it is your last day of freedom before you go in for a life sentence."

I was having emotions coming out of me that I had never had before, and it was something that I did not know how to deal with. All I knew was that I wanted his cock into me at a very rapid pace and wanted him to pound me.

He took his tongue and drove it deep into my hole with an aggression as if he were never going to have pussy again. The thrust of his tongue into my love hole sent waves of pleasure through my body and I felt like a woman that was finally alive; yes, the sex I had in the past few days was amazing, but I needed a man that was unbridled and was not afraid to show me what it was like to be taken by a man possessed. The intense orgasm that was building was becoming more than I could stand and I could not hold back any longer.

"I'm going to cum, I'm cumming, I am fucking fixing to cum my brains out."

"Cum for me, dirty girl. I want to see my dirty girl give her big man all of her juices."

As if by command, I let loose with a

river of juice from my pussy.

He went down on me and licked as much of my love juice as he cold. There was yet again a massive wet spot and we had not even got to the main event of our sexual event.

"I want and need your cock inside me. Fuck fixing the heater. I need your cum in me to fix me." He took his cock and began the process of slowly sticking the head in.

"Fuck me and fuck me as hard as you can." This was all he needed to hear as he did as he was told. He took his cock and shoved its balls deep into my eagerly awaiting pussy, which made me almost cum again with the force of his shove.

"That's right. Fuck me, fuck me like you would if I was the only female in a three-state radius."

The pounding that he was giving my pussy was like nothing I had had in a long while. There was no holding back in his strokes, and I think he knew I was turned on by it. As he continued to fuck me, he got to be more intense and soon made the decision that he was not going to stop until I had a load of his semen deep inside my body. This made me all wet much more.

"Fuck me, fuck my tight hole. I need to be given a lesson in the proper way to treat a man, and you are the one I need it from. Fuck that hole. I bet you are thinking about your wife when you fuck other women, don't you, or are you really looking for someone other than your wife to give your shaft a proper treatment?"

Steve reached down and grabbed both of my nipples as he continued to slide in and out of me. He gave them a tug that made me think that he was going to tear them off of me. He then dug his fingers deep into my flesh mounds, as he began to fuck me with more aggression. The feel of his fingers digging into my tits was actually sending me into more of an orgasm than I had been in quite some time; I wanted him to dig harder.

"Harder, squeeze my tits harder. I want to feel your strength in my tits. Make them fucking pop."

I was like a woman possessed; I was like an addict and sex was my crack. All I wanted was to have the most intense fuck fest; at this point I didn't even care about the fact my heater was broke and I needed to find a job. I was not quitting until my appetite for cock had been filled and I had cum dripping from all of my holes.

He fucked me harder with each thrust. I could feel his balls slamming into the lower part of my pussy and it was driving me over the edge to have the sensation. Again, I felt his member deep inside of me swell in anticipation of an incoming load of jizz.

"Cum in me. I want and need your cum deep inside of me. Fucking show me the type of man you are and plant your seed deep in my wet, hot fucking pussy." With that, he released another large load deep into me. The feel of his hot load was almost as good as the first load he emptied into my mouth. It sent another gush of pussy juices expelling from my freshly fucked fuck hole.

Without hesitation, I got up on all fours and presented my ass for his inspection. The feel of his tongue almost caused me to become unhinged. It was at that moment that I felt his cock use the cum he dumped into my pussy along with my juices that he drove into my asshole; the feel of another man in there was almost worth the freezing that I had done. At this point, I was more sweating than I was freezing. He planted his cock into my ass and began to slowly fuck my hole, sliding in and out and getting more intense with each stoke. I felt him reach around and grab both of my tits; he pulled back on them as if they were horse reins and used them to balance himself while his cock went in and out of me. He was pulling so hard that I thought he was going to pull my tits off me; I had to admit 36DD tits did make for a great way to balance oneself when fucking my tight ass. Lesser men had been in there, and as a result, this made my hole a lot tighter.

"Come, big man. Fuck my ass. You know you like being in that tight hole."

This drove him over the edge and he began to fuck me harder and squeeze my tits that much harder. I was getting off on the fact that I was playing with my pussy while he fucked my ass and squeezed my tits with an anger and furious aggression.

Just when I thought I could not hold out anymore, he pulled back, arching his back and pulling my tits almost to my back, and then I felt the reward of all my efforts. I felt the third and final load of semen enter my eagerly waiting hole. This sent me into an orgasm overload. I released a volcano of juices from my pussy and saw the sheets on the bed become drenched in a massive gush of pussy juice. My ass was covered, and I lifted a couple of fingers to my lips to taste my sweetness that was oozing out of my fuck hole.

"God damn woman, you are quite honestly the best fuck I have ever had. There has not been a woman that has made me feel more like a man than you have. I am more than impressed with you and your expertise."

I fell to the bed exhausted from the furious fuck that I had just had. I was even too weak for a cigarette. I just had my brains fucked out and needed an hour to recover.

I went about my day and Darren came home later that afternoon.

"Damn why does the apartment smell like sex? Who did you fuck this time?"

"The repairman for the heater. I was in the bedroom, he came in and was watching me finger fuck myself, and I had to do something. By the way, I got a call from Heather and she told me that I got hired at the club that she works at. I start on Friday; she also said that they were hiring bouncers."

"By the way, Angela, have you heard anything from Amanda since she left here? She said that she was going to the club to get her things. I hope she is okay."

"I have not heard a word from her. I fear that she might have encountered Anne-Marie. This encounter would not have ended well for her. I hope things are okay. We have a new life that we need to adjust to as this will be a rough new life for you and us as a couple."

AUTHOR'S NOTE

Readers: We want to expand a few of the stories to see where the characters can be explored further. If there are any of the stories that you would like to read more about again, we'd love to hear from you!

Visit our blog at http://www.CarleeShoman.com/
http://www.ChaneyKees.com

Join our newsletter for free exclusive previews
http://www.carleeshoman.com/in
http://www.ChaneyKees.com/in

Follow us on Twitter at
http://www.twitter.com/CarleeShoman
http://www.twitter.com/ChaneyKees

Like our page on Facebook at
http://www.facebook.com/CarleeShoman
http://www.facebook.com/ChaneyKees

Discover our books at major ebook retailers everywhere.